*

"Palma's love of fantasy is no mere exercise in escapism nor a clever game of mirrors, but a way of intuiting the world by freeing oneself from rationalism. His stories demonstrate a perfect tension between poetry, tenderness, and humor."

—*El Mundo*

"[Palma's] works are infused with gifted ideas, unforgettable imagery, and reflections that haunt you long after you've finished the last page. An author of deliciously disquieting short stories."

—*La Razón*

"An amalgam of perfect style, astonishing imagery, and unsettling narrative to chart a disturbing world."

—*ABC Cultural*

"Meticulous, disconcerting, and inspired, Palma exemplifies the very best of short fiction being written in Spanish today."

—*Muface*

PRAISE FOR *The Map of Time*

"*The Map of Time* recalls the science fiction of Wells and Verne, and then turns the early masters on their heads. A brilliant and breathtaking trip through metafictional time."

—Scott Westerfeld,
New York Times bestselling author

"*The Map of Time* is a singularly inventive, luscious story with a core of pure, unsettling weirdness. With unnerving grace and disturbing fantasy, it effortlessly straddles that impossible line between being decidedly familiar and yet absolutely new."

—Cherie Priest, award-winning
author of *Boneshaker*

"Strange and wonderful. Magical and smart. Félix J. Palma has done more than written a wonderful novel, he's concocted a supernatural tour de force. Time travel, tragic love, murder, and mystery all combine in what is nothing short of a surprising, satisfying, and mesmerizing read."

—M.J. Rose, *New York Times*
bestselling author

"A big, genre-bending delight."

—*The Washington Post*

"Palma uses the basic ingredients of steampunk—fantasy, mystery, ripping adventure, and Victorian-era high-tech—to marvelous effect."

—Seattle Times

"Palma makes his U.S. debut with the brilliant first in a trilogy, an intriguing thriller that explores the ramifications of time travel in three intersecting narratives."

—Publishers Weekly
(starred review)

"Readers who embark on the journey . . . will be richly rewarded."

—Booklist
(starred review)

"Lyrical storytelling and a rich attention to detail make this prize-winning novel an enthralling read."

—Library Journal
(starred review)

"Palma is a master of ingenious plotting."

—Kirkus Reviews

THE HEART AND OTHER VISCERA

THE HEART AND OTHER VISCERA

STORIES

PÉLIX J. PALMA

Translated by Nick Caistor *and* Lorenza García

ATRIA PAPERBACK

New York   London   Toronto   Sydney   New Delhi

ATRIA
PAPERBACK

An Imprint of Simon & Schuster, Inc.
1230 Avenue of the Americas
New York, NY 10020

First Atria Paperback edition September 2019

ATRIA PAPERBACK and colophon are trademarks of Simon & Schuster, Inc.

For information about special discounts for bulk purchases, please contact Simon & Schuster Special Sales at 1-866-506-1949 or business@simonandschuster.com.

The Simon & Schuster Speakers Bureau can bring authors to your live event. For more information or to book an event contact the Simon & Schuster Speakers Bureau at 1-866-248-3049 or visit our website at www.simonspeakers.com.

Design by Kyle Kabel

Manufactured in the United States of America

10   9   8   7   6   5   4   3   2   1

Library of Congress Cataloging-in-Publication Data
Names: Palma, Félix J., author.
Title: The heart and other viscera : stories / Félix J. Palma.
Description: First Atria paperback edition. | New York : Atria Paperback, 2019.
Identifiers: LCCN 2018060794 (print) | LCCN 2018061541 (ebook) | ISBN 9781501164057 (eBook) | ISBN 9781501164040 (trade pbk.)
Subjects: LCSH: Palma, Félix J.—Translations into English.
Classification: LCC PQ6666.A3965 (ebook) | LCC PQ6666.A3965 A2 2019 (print) |—DDC 863/.64—dc23
LC record available at https://lccn.loc.gov/2018060794

ISBN 978-1-5011-6404-0
ISBN 978-1-5011-6405-7 (ebook)

Contents

THE HEART AND OTHER VISCERA

Roses against the Wind

Even though I visited him almost every day since I began working two blocks from his home, I knew very little about my grandfather apart from the fact that he loved trains and hated rats.

"You didn't see any rats on the way up, did you?" he would ask me as soon as he opened his eyes and discovered me sitting opposite him on a chair I had dragged in from the kitchen.

His concern about a possible invasion by these sinister vermin was fully justified. My grandfather still lived in the home where he was born, in one of those old-fashioned apartments with high ceilings, huge windows, and doors that folded like accordions. Those walls had seen him be born, totter along its corridors, smoke surreptitiously, write love poems. They had seen him, as it were, prepare himself to face an unimaginable future that noiselessly fell apart at the seams into the present so that now, full of damp patches and as weary as he was, the walls seemed to be contemplating him with unexpected

1

affection as he dozed in his armchair. In this old apartment, where daylight seemed to drag itself in because of the tall modern buildings that had sprung up around it, my grandfather survived on a miserable pension. My father had left him to his own devices a long time ago, as a result of an insult the old man had perpetrated on his wedding day that my father saw as the culmination of the many years of paternal ostracism he had been forced to bear. And yet, my grandfather did not seem at all concerned by his precarious economic situation. If my father had washed his hands of him, he seemed to have washed his hands of the world. A social worker came to clean the apartment and fill his fridge, but I'm not sure if he was even aware of this plump guardian angel assigned to watch over him every Wednesday, as he spent most of the day dozing in his armchair, sleeping with his eyes gently closed and a complicit smile on his lips, as if he knew a secret that was forbidden to the rest of us. Maybe it was the secret of how to escape death, because my grandfather was just over one hundred years old.

If everything around us spoke of the forlorn abandonment of things not even glanced at, the adjacent room was dominated by a huge table that almost entirely filled it. On the table lay the only thing that still captured my grandfather's attention: a gigantic model railway. He'd built it with his own two hands more than half a century ago, and still, even though his fingers had lost much of their dexterity, he continued lovingly adding details: tiny figures or unnecessary trees. It was as if he was reluctant to complete it, perhaps convinced that finishing the model ran parallel with his life, the two things he did not know how to resolve. The entire model was made of wood. A steam engine, the faithful reproduction of a German Adler, plowed tirelessly across a rectangular landscape filled with hills and valleys. Among them, after rummaging in travel books and encyclopedias, my grandfather had dotted the best-known monuments and marvels on the planet. On his model, the world was stripped of all sense of distance and appeared crammed together in an effort at neighborliness that seemed monstrous if one considered the sudden mingling of disparate climes and cultures. With its gleaming dark carriages and red piston rods, the Adler proudly explored an impossible world made up of remnants torn from here and there in the reality that inspired it, as if my grandfather was dreaming of a world that could be seen in its entirety in a single day, at a glance. In his model railway, amid fairy-tale trees and picturesque bridges, the Palace of Versailles rubbed shoulders with Machu Picchu, the Eiffel Tower cast its shadow across the gleaming white expanse of the Taj Mahal, the Great Wall of China folded the Christ statue of Rio de Janeiro in its maternal embrace, Vesuvius strutted in the center of the Red Square, and like gunmen from the Far West, the giants of Easter Island stared their challenge to the buddhas of Angkor Wat.

In a corner of the same room, beneath a window that must have once offered a panorama of the horizon but now revealed only a backstreet choked with garbage, among which every so often a rat's filthy brushstroke could be spotted, was a small table on which my grandfather had laid out his tools. There, nestled among coils of wood shavings, were small pots of paint, knives, and paintbrushes. In the center, like a half-plucked goose, was a book always open to some new monument that would soon make its appearance in a corner of the model. Whenever I saw those extraordinary miniatures, I felt like running to examine my grandfather's hands, hoping to discover there some sign—a phosphorescent aura or something similar—that might help explain how those fingers could imitate reality with such precision. I was always slightly disappointed to see poking out from the worn cuffs of his dressing gown a pair of perfectly ordinary hands shrouded with age, the fingers crooked, the nails yellow. Hands that fit the rest of him: a skinny body, chipped like an old knife, and a cerulean, angular face dominated by a pair of gray eyes that constantly darted about as if they found it impossible to settle on anything.

During my visits, I rarely saw him contemplating his model railway, still less studying it with the smile of satisfaction that I considered more or less obligatory. It would seem my grandfather preferred to sleep, lulled by the purring of the engine on its interminable journey, as it steamed through the motley landscape created by his imagination. At first, I was surprised by this lack of enthusiasm. Then, I realized my grandfather must have every last detail of his creation engraved in his mind, where all the novelties must have appeared several days before they became reality, so that all he had to do was close his eyes to see them. Simply knowing it was there in the next room, indefinitely unfinished, eternally awaiting his additions, my grandfather would smile contentedly, surrounded by an apartment falling to pieces.

"Are you happy with your life, Alberto?" he asked me one afternoon when he came around from his lethargy.

I could scarcely believe my grandfather was capable of asking such an intimate question, the answer to which bordered on the abstract. Or that he might be worried by anything other than the presence of the rats, still less by the life of a grandson whose existence he appeared to summon and dismiss with a blink of his eyes. All I could think as a reply was to shrug my shoulders, as if the whole thing was completely without interest for me. Although, in fact, for several minutes afterward, shielded by the darkness in the room, I tried to come up with an answer to his question. I had just turned thirty-four, and had been working for the same company for the last six years; first, in its old premises and now, for four months, in its new offices on a grand avenue, only ten minutes away from my grandfather's apartment. As a result, for a long while now, my days had been uneventful, tranquil, and monotonous: mornings in the office like an insipid overture that led into lazy evenings of crosswords and coffees, and nights that found me leaning over the balcony with a chilled cocktail and enveloped by the tortured piano music of Tchaikovsky, feeling that there was not much more

I needed, except perhaps to be in the arms of a girl that I had caught sight of on the street, or another one that I had glimpsed on the bus. I had no idea what might make other people happy, but I was sure that the gentle to-and-fro of my days was close to my idea of happiness. Would I really be happier doing other things, leading a life different from this peaceful, secure existence I had unintentionally created for myself? I didn't think I was made for anything else: after all, socializing with my colleagues at the local bar was proof enough that everyone leads similar lives, that the shroud of night covers all these familiar existences, that they are only distinguished by the body wearing a cucumber mask on the far side of the mattress, the urgent sobs of a child, or even sometimes only by a stamp collection or necktie patterns.

And yet, there must have been some kind of dissatisfaction behind the fact that I visited my grandfather every afternoon. Maybe I did so in the secret hope that he would do or say something that would make that day stand out from all the rest. Perhaps I wanted to hear him talk of some battle or other that I knew of only from history books, or for him to plunge me, as befits every grandfather, into an ocean of atrocities and hardships from which I would emerge frozen stiff but ready to reassess my own anodyne existence. Or it might have been to prove what I already suspected, that it made no difference how one lived, because in the end, when our achievements are all behind us, the result is always the same: we are all just trying to fill the empty hours as we wait for death.

The following afternoon, I found my grandfather bent over his worktable. This was a scene I had almost forgotten. The weak evening light dusted his absorbed profile as he busied himself with heaven knows what.

"Come over here," he called out when he heard me arrive.

I walked around the model and stood beside him, expecting to see his knife poised over the carving of yet another monument to add to his scaled-down world. But what I found when my grandfather withdrew his bony hands with a magician's theatrical gesture wasn't a monument but the tiny figure of a gray-suited man carrying a leather briefcase. I studied it in astonishment, admiring every detail: the folds of his suit, the buckles on the briefcase, the twisted knot on the necktie, even the infinite humanity with which in four brushstrokes he had managed to capture the expression of tedium on his face. A shiver ran down my spine when I realized that the little figure I had been examining for almost a minute was me.

Once I recovered from the shock, the shame of seeing myself portrayed so exactly in this diminutive copy, from my gray suit to my briefcase and my constantly twisted tie, made my cheeks burn. Was the image I had of myself so different that it took me a whole minute to recognize myself? I was face to-face with the sad reality, the uninspiring image that my grandfather, and with him probably the rest of the world, had of me. This was me, an insignificant little man with an eternally resigned expression, no more than a speck of dust in a universe that belonged to others.

The placid smile on my grandfather's lips contradicted any sense of judgment. This was not a criticism, even if when I recognized myself in the figurine I had felt that treacherous thrust of a knife in my back. No, it was a gift. A gift my grandfather had decided to offer me without my being able to guess the reason why. Still smiling with an expression that gave his mouth a frail look, like a sweet made by nuns, my grandfather picked up the figure and went over to the model railway. He halted the Adler, lifted the roof off of one of the carriages, and very carefully sat me inside it.

As he did so, I could not help but recall my father and see, as though I had been there in person, his wedding day, when, drunk on wine, he had risen from his chair and accused my grandfather of not bringing any gift, in reality seeking to reproach him for many other things he had neither the wish nor the strength to list. He himself had told me hundreds of times how, in the silence caused by his outburst, my grandfather had replied that if he wanted to see his gift, all he had to do was go home with him. My father had immediately taken him at his word and, not giving a damn about disrupting the reception, had almost dragged my mother and most of the guests with him to come and stand in this very room, in front of what in those days was a much less cluttered model railway, still demanding his gift like an insistent, spoiled child. My grandfather pointed to one of the train carriages. Inside, my astonished parents could see two painted wooden figures, perfect copies of themselves. My father took this as an insult, one more in the long list of veiled offenses that had marred the relationship between father and son. This was the worst one of all, as it seemed aimed not only at him, but also at the woman he loved.

My father had stoically put up with my grandfather's numerous outrages, his lack of interest and affection toward him, his exclusive dedication to that dratted model railway, where now, in a clumsy joke only he could understand, he found himself included. But on this occasion, my grandfather had gone too far. It took my father several minutes to react, as if he was somehow taking stock, taking his time to draw out from within himself all the hatred that had been accumulating for years. When he was ready, he stopped the locomotive with a furious swipe of his hand and picked up the insulting figures. Staggering with wine and rage, the tails of his morning coat giving him the air of a swallow in flight, he rushed into the bathroom and threw them down the toilet. The watery roar of the cistern seemed to go on for hours, engulfing the dumbstruck guests in a horror show. That gesture from my father caused the frail thread that still united him and his father to snap. It was as if from that moment on they turned their backs on each other, as in a duel for their honor, so that they paced through life refusing to acknowledge the tug of the blood bond that they shared.

My father repeated the story many times over the years. In time, it began to lose much of its dramatic effect, so that in the end it seemed to me no more than a misunderstanding played out in front of too big an audience; a stupid argument between two people who were too different to understand each other. There was no asking my father to reconsider and make peace with my grandfather, despite the fact that his life was drawing to a close. Perhaps that was why I went to see him every afternoon, thinking I was keeping his loneliness at bay, when in reality I was trying to scare mine away. That was also why I put on my best smile when the locomotive moved off again, taking me with it in its bowels.

That night, while waiting for sleep to overcome me, I thought about my grandfather's strange gift, that curious way of his of making a globetrotter out of a grandson who had never left his own neighborhood. I thought it was amusing to be traveling around the world while lying in my bed. I imagined myself taking the place of my tiny replica, speeding through a toy reality that would transform the moment I decided to suspend my disbelief and accept the laws of the model railway. I saw myself seated in that old-fashioned carriage, imagining the gentle rocking of the Adler in my bones and trying to visualize the landscapes and monuments parading nonstop before my eyes. The Champs-Élysées, the Süleymaniye Mosque, the Atomium. I fell asleep, fantasizing of those remote places I had only ever seen in photographs, and went on doing so in my dreams. Upon awakening, I could sense the afterglow of exotic visions, the nebulous recollection of things I had never seen.

I reached the office brandishing a radiant smile. I knew that I had only traveled in my dreams, but it had seemed so lifelike, so real, that it was not hard to fool myself into thinking I had really been in all those places, the memories of which still fluttered in my mind like extremely fragile butterflies. All morning, I couldn't get the image of the little figure out of my mind. I was overwhelmed by an odd nostalgia that occasionally seemed like envy, imagining him traveling tirelessly around and around the model railway, seeing things I never would, even if it was only a make-believe world.

However, I did not understand the real gift my grandfather had given me until almost the end of my day, when, weary of so many idiotic reports, I closed my eyes to rest. All of a sudden, I found myself in a railway carriage, lulled by its rattling wheels and blinded by the stream of light flooding the compartment. Terrified, I opened my eyes once more, only to find myself back in my small office with the hum of the computer and embalmed by a chilly October's leaden light. Had I been the victim of a hallucination? Taking a deep breath, I settled in my chair, holding on tightly to the arms, and tried again, this time closing my eyelids deliberately slowly. I found myself in the compartment once more, seated by the window. There was no doubt it was a carriage pulled by the Adler. The compartment was lit by oil lamps, and my nostrils were filled with the smell of burning coal. Outside the window, the castle at Elsinore rose like an apparition, wrapped in a shroud of fog, with its fairy-tale spires and high redbrick walls, where Hamlet was struggling with his phantoms. I opened my eyes again: I was back in the all-too-familiar setting of my office.

Everything was the same all around me. There was no longer any smell of coal or oil. In the background, I could hear the clamor of telephones, the banging of fingers on keyboards. And yet all I had to do was close my eyes for all of this to disappear, and for another reality to take its place. I tried to relax. I mustn't allow myself to be carried away either by panic or by the excitement of this discovery. I waited patiently for my workday to finish, and then, back at my apartment, after fortifying myself with a glass of wine, I sat on the sofa to continue with my experiments. I was in Berlin, Istanbul, the Alps. I discovered that all I had to do was lower my eyelids to be transported into my tiny wooden double, to see with his eyes and no longer with my own. With no more effort than that, I could pass from my insignificant reality to the one my grandfather had built; between the two there was no more than a momentary sense of vertigo, an instant when I swung in the air, too short to feel anything worse than the fleeting anxiety acrobats must experience as they fly toward the hands of their colleague.

I spent that evening, and many more thereafter, traveling the world from the threadbare sofa in my living room. The crosswords piled up on the table while I greeted the floating houses on the canals of Amsterdam, wished for love by tossing a coin into the Fontana di Trevi, or fell head over heels for a Malaysian girl playing with a turtle on a beach in China. At nightfall, I would go out onto the balcony and stare at the snowy peak of Mont Blanc, the national lottery building, the multicolored temple of Toshogu, the kiosk of the association for the blind, the man in the cobbler's setting off a stampede of antelopes when he pulled the noisy shutter down. And as the colors drained from my neighborhood, I would prepare a pot of coffee that I would drink amid the aroma of lilies in a Japanese garden, followed by the elegant beauty of the Acropolis, and ending at Westminster Abbey. The bite of a hermit crab on a Greek beach still stung as I caressed the plumage of a toucan in the Amazon rain forest. I wore a Naga warrior's bearskin-lined headdress decorated with wild boar's teeth, and came across a precious gemstone as I sifted through mud in the mines of Ratnapura. At night, when my eyes were closed by the will of Morpheus, I also traveled ceaselessly: Berne, Montreal, Dublin, a kaleidoscope of cities covered in clouds of steam, a feast of monuments and architectures that swallowed one another up and procreated at the whim of the tracks, giving rise to delirious hybrids, aberrations of a bastardized history of which I retained only a vague awareness upon waking. When I took a shower, I could not help but be aware of the pleasant tiredness of someone who has been on a long journey, a slight aftertaste of alien experiences as the water soothed my muscles, a trace of unknown perfumes mixing with the smell of my shaving cream, the caress of a distant breeze as I did up my tie.

This extraordinary way of traveling soon became an addiction. Before long, it wasn't enough for me to use it as an escape from my daily routine, to lessen the boredom of my evenings.

I started to feel an irrepressible hunger to see the world, a desire for new places that forced me to set off even during office hours. Every morning, I worked without any breaks and completed my reports with unheard-of diligence, so that by midday I had nothing left to do. I would shut myself in one of the bathroom stalls and escape to the temple at Karnak, to Mount Rushmore, the beaches of Sri Lanka. Later, I would leave the office as stealthily as someone hiding a secret, feeling overwhelmingly transparent whenever a work colleague's eyes rested on me. Despite everything, I also couldn't help feeling an immense sense of pity toward them. After returning from New Guinea, where, daubed in mud and wearing a bird-of-prey mask, I had taken part in a ritual battle against the spirits, my colleagues seemed painfully ordinary, without depth or color, satisfied with a life that was as narrow as a coffin to me. A life that for many years had been mine, where there was nothing beyond what could be seen or touched.

I was enjoying myself so much, gorging myself on landscapes the way others binged on sweets, that I had barely paused to reflect on the causes and consequences of those astral journeys. But one evening, after returning from my enthralled contemplation of the grass roof of the church at Funningur, I saw myself reflected in the windowpane. My drowsy posture on the sofa seemed to me identical to the one my grandfather adopted for most of the day. This led me to wonder whether I was the only one who traveled this way, or whether my grandfather had known about it for years. That would explain a lot of things; it would solve the mystery of an entire life. I ran to his apartment and searched the model railway in the hope of also finding a diminutive replica of my grandfather. None of the tiny figures seemed to represent him. This inexplicable absence of his own double came as a huge disappointment. Did it mean my grandfather was immune to the magic of the model, that for him it was no more than a pointless amusement, that he was unaware of everything I was experiencing?

This was what I thought until one evening, as I was rummaging in a sideboard drawer for his cough mixture, my eyes caught one of the portraits standing on top of it. It showed my grandfather as a young man, a stocky, sinewy lad smiling shyly at the camera while adjusting a checkered cloth cap. I stared at it a long while without being able to grasp what was so familiar about it. As soon as I did, I ran to the model railway. There, on the side of a hill, I found what I was looking for: the figure of a robust young man wearing a checkered cap. The hill gave way to the extraordinary Saint Basil's Cathedral, and I realized that, curled up on his armchair in the living room, my grandfather must be agreeing with Ivan the Terrible, who had ordered that the eyes of its architect should be gouged out so that he would never again create anything so beautiful.

I brought in a chair from the kitchen and sat in my usual spot opposite him, but I looked at him in a very different light. No longer was he a poor old man, unable to stay awake until his hour arrived. Now my grandfather seemed to me a compulsive hedonist, a devoted sybarite who all these years had the world at his feet. He had cut himself off from everything, had given himself over to pure pleasure, regardless of the price he paid. Possibly, he had his doubts before he sacrificed what might be called his corporal existence; perhaps he had them when he understood that this would also ruin most of his son's as well. Or maybe he didn't have a choice—once he had tried it, he couldn't leave it alone—and maybe sharing this treasure with his son and the woman he loved was the only way he could find to resolve his weakness.

My grandfather had offered his son the most rewarding gift anyone could possibly give him, but my father had seen only two ridiculous small figures, and he had thrown them down the drain. That same night, I had dinner with my parents to confirm what I already knew, to glimpse once more, beneath their impeccable manners, their unsophisticated happiness as a well-off couple, that dark shadow that had troubled me since childhood and whose origin I finally understood. By pulling the toilet chain, my father had rejected heaven and embraced hell. Now I knew the reason for the clouded look in their eyes. I understood all the pointless visits to psychoanalysts, my father's frequent bouts of insomnia, my mother's desperate need to wrap herself in a cocoon of glittering luxury. I knew now that they were suffering a punishment they did not understand, sharing a sickness they found impossible to combat, and that they were unable to dream as they slept. They lived without understanding why when they closed their eyes all they could see was an ocean of turbulent, muddy waters; a horrific, putrid world, a sewer they were condemned to descend into every night.

Unlike my father, I had understood my grandfather's gift. I accepted it as a blessing, with infinite thanks. Those journeys were a paradise to me. But there was something missing. And like Adam, I also begged the creator of all this for a female companion.

"I don't want to go on traveling alone," I dared confess to him one evening, kneeling beside him in a woolly silence disturbed only by the hypnotic thrum of the Adler locomotive on the tracks in the adjacent room. "Beauty is increased if it's shared."

My grandfather did not reply. He still had his eyes shut, which I preferred; I probably would never have revealed my feelings in this way if he had been looking at me. But I knew from experience that my grandfather would hear my voice floating over all the places he had imagined, and so I described as best I could the woman I desired, so that he would have no problem creating her in wood. I told him that she should be as delicate as a teardrop, with eyes like mint among weeds, and a slender body so light that the slightest puff of wind could steal her from me. I rounded off her portrait in a voice aching with desire and filled with melancholy. Then I fled from my grandfather's apartment feeling slightly ashamed, as if he had discovered me masturbating. I spent all the next morning tortured by doubts, wondering if my grandfather's fingers were at that very moment giving my wish a shape, or whether on the contrary my request had seemed to him an impertinence he had no wish to satisfy. The moment work was over, I walked to his apartment full of expectation. My grandfather was dozing in his armchair. I went into the adjoining room to look at the model railway, afraid that my plea had not been heeded. Tears filled my eyes when in the carriage of the Adler I came upon a female figure who would put an end to my solitude.

As soon as I closed my eyes that night, I could smell a woman's perfume struggling to overpower the smell of oil in the compartment. She was sitting beside me, and I could admire her face while the green of her irises reflected a rushing kaleidoscope of the wonders of the world: the Parthenon rising above the walls of the Kremlin, Notre Dame Cathedral followed instantly by the Blue Mosque of Istanbul, then Prague, Helsinki, and Vienna crashing against the train window like machine-gun bullets. The entire world was ours: mankind's achievements and the caprices of nature, jumbled together in a unique, demented geography, an itinerary devised according to my grandfather's wishes.

That night, and many of those that followed, I became an improbable seducer, a dramatic Don Juan who could call on all the most beautiful backdrops in the world to win the heart of the woman he loved. I invited her to a crazy menu made up of cheese fondue with truffles, Hungarian goulash, and Peking-style duck, all of it washed down with a French sparkling wine laid down in a Rheims wine cellar. We smiled at each other from behind Venetian masks. We took each other in Oslo. And in Tierra del Fuego, like two silly lovers, we planted roses against the wind.

Every morning, when I walked through the lobby of my office building, she gazed at me in a way she never had before. Beautiful and dazed-looking, perched behind the receptionists' desk, she watched me come in and go over to the elevators without taking her eyes off me. I had been in love with her for months. According to her badge, her name was Celia Riquelme, and she was not born of my rib (my bones didn't have that much imagination) but from the last round of new hires. Although previously she had not paid me the slightest attention, for some days now, she registered my arrival as though spellbound. She was obviously wondering who this unremarkable guy was that she dreamed of every night with oneiric punctuality, the prophet of a wondrous world where a hunter seemed to have painstakingly shot all the tigers one by one, and torn up all the nettles. With my back to her, I could hear the telephone ring without her making any effort to pick it up. I could tell she was staring at me as if trying to solve a riddle, her mind still full of the tumultuous sensations of a crazy night that had never existed, in which the lips of the stranger now waiting for the elevator had slid like a slimy slug's all over her dappled body, specially doused for the occasion in Armenian brandy. And occasionally, when I had to go out for some reason, I would find her leaning back in her chair, her eyes gently closed and a contented smile on her face. This was when I realized that, like me, she was no longer afraid and had learned to enjoy my grandfather's gift without asking herself any questions. She gave in to it with all the blind trust of a little girl in her father's arms, enjoying the twists and turns in midair without ever thinking those hands could let her fall. She loved me; she was loving me well ahead of reality. Every night, we gave ourselves to each other despite the fact that we had never actually touched, and I was in no hurry to transfer this joyous love to our insipid world, where it could crumble at the slightest obstacle.

It was then that I discovered, from so often pleasurably studying the model railway, the deceitful, miniature world where our romance could blossom, that the figures moved around in it. Every evening, I found them in different places in the landscape. I didn't want to ask my grandfather if it was he who moved them, if he was the one who decided on a whim each morning what was to be the backdrop to our dreams. What did one more mystery matter if we lived in a gingerbread house in an enchanted wood?

Those were happy, beautiful days. But we soon discovered that their destiny was like that of the roses we were so desperate to grow in Patagonia, tributes to a vanished beauty always swept away by the cruel wind in the end. It happened on a weekday morning like any other, when the Adler was steaming happily through paddy fields of rice. Celia and I had transported ourselves while at work and were sitting inside the locomotive, holding hands, enjoying the green spectacle outside the window, when a sudden pestilence invaded our compartment. It was a nauseous, unpleasant smell that we had no time to identify. Suddenly, the locomotive seemed to be jolted forward, sending a shock wave through the whole train. Then we heard the sound of wild steps, as if of something powerful, huge, and unimaginable rushing toward us. I clutched Celia's hand just as the roof of our carriage was smashed open with a monstrous crash. Among the splinters, I could make out a damp darkness bristling with fangs coming toward us.

I opened my eyes at once. And found myself in a bathroom stall, believing I was safe from whatever had burst into the kindly world of the model railway. A second later, I was proven wrong when an intense pain in the pit of my stomach made me fall to the floor, writhing like a heroin addict. I bit my lips to stop myself crying out, fighting to overcome the terrible pain even as I noticed blood running down my throat. The stabbing sensations came and went, like arbitrary, absentminded bites. Something was savaging my wooden double, and although I was feeling only a pallid reflection of the suffering, a kind of scaled-down martyrdom, I realized with a shudder of panic that this torture could easily end in the loss of a limb or even my head. How would that be reflected in the real world? How would it affect me? Best not to know. At all costs, I had to prevent that from happening. The only chance I had was to take advantage of the intervals between bites, when I could perhaps walk or crawl, to try to reach the model railway.

I staggered out of the bathroom, reeled down the corridor, trying not to attract attention, and collapsed inside the elevator the moment the doors opened. I pressed the buttons like a blind man. In the lobby, I was confronted with a dreadful surprise: surrounded by alarmed onlookers, Celia was writhing, convulsing on the floor like someone possessed. That painful sight gave me the sharpest bite of all. Feeling guilty, I rushed out of the building, knowing there was nothing I could do for her there. The only way I could help was by reaching my grandfather's apartment as quickly as possible.

I ran through the streets like a madman. Every so often, a searing pain hurled me to the ground, and I had to wait for it to cease in order to continue, even though I knew that the fact that I was freed for the moment from those phantom jaws only meant that they were toying with Celia instead. By the time I reached my grandfather's building, I was panting, crumpled, and aching in a thousand different places. I more or less crawled up the stairs. With no time to search for the keys, I gave the rotten door a kick, and it burst open. I lurched down the gloomy hallway, and found my grandfather fast asleep on the sofa, oblivious to everything. My head spinning, I ran into the adjoining room. The sight of the model railway was heart-rending. Numerous little figures lay destroyed and smashed in a winding path to the center, where, in the midst of the train's shattered remains, lurked an enormous rat. Its snorting muzzle was poking about in one of the upturned carriages. Hearing me enter the room, it left whatever it was doing and turned its head in my direction. We stared at each other for a few seconds, as if sizing each other up. Among the wreck of the carriage, I could make out our two replicas, covered in viscous saliva and teeth marks but still relatively intact. The rat's tiny eyes gleamed like pinheads, full of that vivid intelligence that for some reason (perhaps because they don't talk) we always attribute to animals. But it was enough for me to whirl my arms to reduce it to its condition as a rodent and send it running. The rat scurried frantically all over the railway, sweeping away everything in its path, searching for an escape route from that labyrinth raised too high above the floor. It eventually found one in the kitchen chair I used to sit on every evening to admire our miniature world, and which I had forgotten to replace the last time I had been there. But before it leaped off the table, the rat had time to snatch a final victim, a solitary figure it found on its way—the replica of a young globetrotter in a checkered cap. I gave an anguished shout and tried to block its path, but the rat scuttled between my legs and disappeared down the dark corridor.

Horrified, I fixed my eyes on my grandfather, who was still asleep in the other room. For an instant, it looked as if nothing was going to happen, that there was no kind of link between him and the snatched figure. I hoped against hope that this was true, that the nightmare that had been about to destroy Celia and me would respect him. Then the convulsions started. My grandfather suddenly opened his eyes, but it was too late. Terrified, he sought out my own eyes, unable to comprehend the lacerating pain in his insides. He stretched out his hand to me, seeking a help that no one could give him. I stared at him, impotent. All of a sudden, he sat up violently on the sofa and his skinny body began a grotesque dance full of impossible jerks and contortions. Then something ruthlessly cruel pulled at the top of his head, his neck like a violin string tightened by a sadist, until finally there was the sharp, macabre crack of a life being snapped. After that, he lay very still, in such a relaxed posture on the sofa it looked as if he had fallen asleep once more after the tumult. Only his staring eyes and the scarlet tears sliding down from the corners of his mouth told me he would never wake up again.

I went slowly over to him and gently closed his eyes. Even though that gesture was no longer the passport to traveling through the fabulous world of the model railway, but to explore a much darker, colder, and unimaginable one from which one never returned. I stroked his hair and imagined him seated in the carriage of his Adler, crossing a gloomy landscape and acknowledging the greetings from his friendly phantoms. But I also saw him steaming through a world full of color, trees laden with fruit, unlikely birds, and crystalline streams. Who could tell?

I returned to the other room and surveyed the model. With his death, my grandfather's great work was at an end. No fingers would be able to continue to complete it, adding marvels to that miniature world where my parents had found misfortune and I had found happiness.

I struck a match and brought its flame to the tiny pile of wood that had once been the Tower of Pisa. Backing away, I watched as the flames spread over the model, turning its dreams to ashes, and looked down at the two battered figures I had managed to rescue from the fire. What future was in store for them now that they only had an absurd, cold world far bigger than them to count on? I suddenly felt the fierce breath of the flames on my face and couldn't help feeling terribly alone and vulnerable. Like those roses that Celia and I planted in Patagonia, tokens of hope that the wind tore to shreds all too soon.

The Karenina Syndrome

All families, rich and poor, have secrets to hide. Even the ordinary ones who do not reside in palaces nor are crammed into hovels, but who dwell in so-called single-family homes, those architectural consolations designed for people with some money, though not a lot. The Crespillos, my in-laws, lived in one of these: a semidetached, two-story building with an elongated garage, a balcony about which the bougainvillea had patiently entwined itself, and a minuscule patch of lawn, scarcely bigger than a bath mat, where, should the need arise, only small secrets could be interred.

Despite being married to Eva for five years, I still hadn't managed to wriggle out of the customary Sunday lunches at her parents' house. As in an Aeschylean tragedy, our Sunday get-togethers were based upon a fatal chain of events: beer, lunch, and coffee. Of these three acts—which I accepted like a penance, as if this was the price to pay for the miracle of Eva placing her voluptuous, streamlined swimmer's body next to mine every night—the most dreadful was without a doubt the first: that interminable hour when, while my wife helped her mother finish making lunch, I was forced to wander round the house, left to my own devices, dreading the moment when Eva would place a couple of beers in my hands and with a knowing smile send me forth, like a virgin offered in sacrifice, into the den my father-in-law had made for himself in the garage.

That Sunday was no different. Even though the standing invitation was for two o'clock, Eva rushing me so we wouldn't be late, lunch was never ready. We found Angeline, my mother-in-law, bustling about the kitchen as usual in her Sunday best. Seeing us appear, she left red smudges on both our cheeks that remained there like scars, then launched into an account of the extravagant woes she had suffered that week, all the while keeping a close eye on the stove. Pausing in the doorway, unsure whether to enter that temple where a religion of sauces and spices was practiced that was alien to me, I observed my mother-in-law's frenetic activity. Clad in an apron and high heels, she briskly stirred a boiling pot as she kept an eye on the lamb in the oven, whisked eggs for the cake, and dressed an enormous salad. It was as if she were preparing for the arrival of a company of battle-weary soldiers, who would wolf all that down with brutal efficiency. Eva immediately found something to occupy herself with, and mother and daughter began one of those mystifyingly banal conversations that I only half listened to, doing my best to hide my despair as I imagined our lives endlessly intertwining, like the stubborn branches of the bougainvillea smothering the balcony. Noticing me, Eva plucked two beers from the fridge and invited me to go and join my father-in-law, despite me having explained to her on several occasions that no spark of friendship would ever be ignited between her father and me, not even a faint glimmer of appreciation, regardless of how many beers I brought him.

My father-in-law, Jacob, had created a small workshop inside the garage, where he frittered away his retirement. With his gleaming tools assembled on hooks along the walls like an arsenal of machetes, my father-in-law attempted to unravel the mysteries of DIY, taming unruly pieces of wood according to the instruction manuals he had amassed throughout his tedious life as an accountant. Although I had never heard him speak about the hobby he was nurturing in the secluded sanctity of the garage, I suspected that what attracted him to it was the possibility of using his hands to create something concrete after years of grappling with abstract figures. Now, at last, Jacob was able to create something tangible, something with weight, texture, and even smell, which would embody his labors. That day, like so many others, I descended the precipitous stairs leading to the garage, making as much noise as I could to alert him to my intrusion, all the while cursing my parents for having had the effrontery to perish in an airplane crash, leaving me with a macabre picnic at the cemetery as my only alternative to those Sunday lunches with my in-laws. I found Jacob hunched over his workbench, busying himself with what appeared to be the rudiments of a birdhouse, or a shoeshine box. In short, another of those objects I would never see again. It was as if as soon as they were finished my father-in-law dismantled them, like those Tibetan monks who destroy their sand mosaics to symbolize the death and rebirth of the universe. Or perhaps his labors produced only half-formed progeny, wooden monstrosities, which he disposed of in his neighbors' trash cans at night, disowning all connection with them. Whatever the case, at the age of nearly seventy, my father-in-law had decided to spend his dwindling energies on these homemade projects with the residual strength that kept him going long after he had paid his dues to society.

I said hello and held out one of the beers. As usual, Jacob didn't bother to conceal his irritation at my presence in his sanctuary. Looking askance at me, he gave a curt response, making no move to relieve me of the beer. My father-in-law was a man of medium stature, with sad eyes that seemed to be in perpetual mourning, a thick shock of silver hair, and a skinny frame that looked as if it were made of intertwined canes. Not wanting to slink off like an obsequious butler, I set the beer down on an uncluttered corner of the table and made some remark about the weather, in what I knew would be a vain attempt to strike up a conversation. Jacob gave his usual clipped responses, as he had from the very first day Eva introduced us, when it became obvious after half an hour that our communication would never be easy. Not because we detested each other, but simply because, just as certain materials are poor conductors, the current of conversation doesn't flow between some people. We were doomed to an eternal exchange of terse, guarded comments. When I could think of nothing more to say about the weather, about the winter sun shining in some distant place, far from the garage where my father-in-law and I were moldering, I fell silent. Jacob took this as a signal to resume his tinkering, thus putting an end to the meaningless dialogue we were obliged to engage in every Sunday. I stood for a while, observing his hands, which were a mass of cuts and scratches. There was the proof, written in his own blood, that Jacob didn't have the slightest talent for DIY. Still, he was better at crafting than at interpersonal relations, for if I had one consolation it was that my father-in-law's indifference to me extended to the entire universe. Even to Eva and Angeline, to whom, as far as I could see, he was equally hostile. More than once, I had caught him looking at the two women with contempt, as if they had caused him some terrible affront. And yet, according to what Eva told me, neither she nor her mother had done anything to upset him. The most likely explanation was that lengthy exposure to the verbose Angeline had caused him to relinquish speech, I thought mockingly, before realizing that, in fact, there needn't be any specific reason; some people simply become embittered with age, until all of a sudden, their nearest and dearest forget that once upon a time they were different. Not wishing to give too much thought to something I didn't really care about, I took a swig of beer and said goodbye to Jacob with a vague wave of my hand, to which he didn't respond.

Back upstairs, I began roaming about the house, steering clear of the kitchen lest the two women demand a report on what had transpired in the inhospitable garage. As I wandered from room to room, I found myself wondering whether my father-in-law had played any part in the abrupt disappearance of my wife's ex-fiancé, Alfred, who had decided to jump ship a few weeks before their wedding, leaving his motives for doing so a mystery that Eva had never managed to solve. I found it hard to imagine Jacob pursuing a campaign of intimidation. It was more sensible to assume that this Alfred fellow had fled after realizing that as long as his unfriendly father-in-law was still around, relations with his future family weren't going to be particularly harmonious. Whatever the case, I had no intention of stirring up the past, let alone throwing in the towel like my predecessor. Besides, there was Angeline, who, although she treated me with the same mawkish sentimentality she would a backward child or a crippled dog, at least didn't appear to see me as a demonic creature attempting to infiltrate her family with some dastardly purpose in mind.

My journey took me to the dining room, where I found the table draped with the familiar white linen tablecloth, on which the plates and cutlery had been laid out with the precision of a Japanese garden. I calculated that in approximately twenty minutes my mother-in-law and my wife would start serving lunch and decided to spend the time perusing my in-laws' meager book collection. As is the norm for the majority of people who aren't habitual readers, this was made up of a mishmash of titles, some of them gifts, others special offers from book clubs. More than once, I had snatched up one of those volumes and pretended to leaf through it with interest when Angeline or Eva swept into the room carrying some dish or other. That day, all I wanted to do was lean back in an armchair and watch the two women come and go with a lack of interest bordering on disdain—like one who considers himself above good and evil, and dining with his in-laws. However, when I thought I heard a noise in the corridor, I hurriedly plucked the nearest book from the shelf. It was an old edition of *Anna Karenina*, Leo Tolstoy's great work; a dreadfully tattered volume, as faded as the proverbial flower, which I had always skipped over, convinced it was a source of infectious diseases. Overcoming my revulsion, I opened it at random, even as I listened for the slightest sound emanating from the corridor. It was then I discovered the letter.

I contemplated it nervously. It was a folded piece of yellowing paper, covered with impeccable handwriting, which made me think it had been copied from a first draft. The opening line sprang at me from the page: *My darling, I am writing this in an attempt to steal your heart.* My pulse quickened as I realized it was a love letter. A love letter someone had forgotten or concealed there for some reason. One shouldn't read another's private correspondence, and yet curiosity always triumphs over the pangs of conscience, especially after such a promising beginning. Keeping an eye on the corridor, I unfolded the letter, fearing it might disintegrate in my hands, proving it was simply an illusion designed to lessen my boredom. The author of the missive, whoever he or she was, continued in the same impassioned tone: *This evening I'm using the opportunity of returning your wonderful book to conceal my soul within its pages. I want you to know that all those nights when we dared to finally abandon ourselves to our desire, caring for nothing save our own enjoyment, have made me the happiest person alive. Often, as if it was part of the game, we would whisper words of love to each other, but now I am starting to realize that, deep down, neither of us was playing. I wanted you the first time I saw you, and now that I've had you, I want no one else.* The author went on to refer to their amorous encounters in detail: the taste of the other's beloved skin, smells and moans, kisses and caresses that would be etched on the author's memory forever, all written in the tragic tone of an impossible love—as if whoever wrote it felt at once defeated and emboldened by the enormous sacrifice life was demanding in order for their love to survive. As I followed the lines falteringly, I could feel my heart begin to leap about in my chest, partly because of the mixture of excitement and embarrassment I felt at having stumbled on the unbridled emotions of a stranger, and partly for fear that Eva or her mother would suddenly appear in the dining room, surprising me in that irreverent act. I had reached the final paragraph when I heard the clack of heels advancing along the corridor: *But having you for those nights isn't enough: I want you for the rest of my life. What do we care what the world or other people think, my love? Be bold, my darling; let*

this feeling grow and overwhelm us. Come with me, far away.
The letter ended with a rather childish proposition that they
elope: *I'll wait for you at midnight, at the place where we first
kissed. Please don't fail me. I shall be waiting for you, ready
to fight for what I love. If you don't come, I will never touch
you again.*

I scarcely had time to hide the letter in the book and
replace it on the shelf before my mother-in-law swept into
the room with the lamb on a serving platter. I greeted her
with a foolish grin, aware that if she were to notice my flushed
cheeks, the sweat beading my brow, and my rigid posture,
she would realize something was afoot. However, Angeline
simply returned my smile, placed the lamb on the table, and
informed her husband with an operatic yell that lunch was
served. My father-in-law took his time to emerge from the
crypt, resigned to sharing his table with mortals. During those
mealtimes, it was the women who shouldered the burden
of the conversation. Angeline talked around and around in
circles, like someone grinding coffee; Eva struggled to make
herself heard, raising her voice until she almost went hoarse,
while Jacob blinked behind his impenetrable silence, observing with a heavy heart those irrelevant beings, who hadn't a
clue which sandpaper to use on which type of wood, and I
nodded mechanically at everything, like those silly dogs that
used to adorn the dashboards of cars. Every now and then,
my mother-in-law would shoot an unexpected question at me
and I would respond as best and as rapidly as I could, realizing

I had a minimum amount of time before she resumed her meandering monologue.

That day, however, disturbed by the letter, I could only pretend to concentrate on the lamb. I avoided lifting my gaze from my plate, fearing my mother-in-law might read in my eyes that I had just stumbled upon her secret. At the same time, I took every opportunity when she wasn't looking to contemplate the object of that feverish prose. Angeline always reminded me of a handful of jewelry wrapped in a twist of brown paper. She had never struck me as beautiful, either now—at fifty-something, her thin face grotesquely plastered in makeup—or in her youth—when she was a slender, timid girl, as could be seen from the photographs dotted throughout the house. Yet someone had adored that woman. Someone had written that her hands were like a pair of anxious doves, that her kisses tasted of rainwater, and that he would never forget her caresses. Incredible as it might seem to me, that tiresome woman, with her exquisitely vulgar manners, had unleashed a raging passion in some man. She had ignited him from within, made him roar with desire. She had permitted him to discover true love, the love some of us only know through novels, the love for which we are told we must abandon everything. Inspired by the words of the mysterious author, I couldn't help but see in this woman sitting before me, greedily devouring her lamb, a touch of beauty I had never noticed before, as if Angeline were one of those abstract paintings that only appear sublime when the artist explains them to us. However, not only had my mother-in-law suddenly become more beautiful, she had also grown in stature before my eyes. The past had lent her another dimension, proving that even the dullest people can contain secret compartments. Angeline hadn't always been this fifty-something-year-old woman balancing a leg of lamb on a platter every Sunday; she'd had a previous life that contained at least one episode worthy of being lived. But who was this rapturous lover? I wondered. I had heard Eva say on numerous occasions that her parents started dating when they were very young, which meant that the author of the letter must have appeared on the scene when my mother-in-law was already engaged, or possibly even married. That would explain the letter's tragic, urgent tone. Could he have been a mutual friend? It was obvious that Angeline had never gone to that rendezvous. For some strange reason, my mother-in-law had chosen Jacob, that melancholy man devoted to DIY. Lifting a morsel of lamb to my lips, I openly stared at her. Did she live with the grief of not having chosen the other man? Did she dream of another's hands caressing her at night? Or perhaps she was proud of herself for having stayed with Jacob, and that sustained her? The realization that I might be the only other person there who knew of the existence of this lover gave me a sudden sense of power. I told myself that one day I might be able to use that information to my own benefit, even if just then I couldn't think of how. I longed to give my mother-in-law a knowing look, but she was still taken up with her own chatter. It dawned on me then that the author had never mentioned Angeline by name, referring to her only as "my love" or "my darling," which offered no clue as to the gender of the beloved. Nor were the descriptions of her body explicit enough to reveal that. Could the letter have been addressed to Jacob, whose hands were two doves, anxious to build their own dovecote?

However, when we stood up from the table and moved into the tiny living room to begin the third act, I was assailed by an even greater doubt. The fact that the letter was still inside the book might seem to be an oversight, and yet it could equally mean that the person it was addressed to didn't know it was there. What if the author had merely returned the book, trusting that its owner would flick through it before putting it away, perhaps to reread a couple of passages they might have talked about? I looked at my in-laws, sitting far apart, waiting for Eva to finish serving the coffee. There couldn't have been two people more unalike. I wondered if they hadn't stayed together simply because one of them didn't know about the existence of the letter offering them the chance to change their life. If so, what was I supposed to do? Was it my duty to tell them about my discovery?

I contemplated the shelf next to the television, which my father-in-law had just switched on and would now gaze at indifferently until he was allowed to return to his workshop. *Anna Karenina* stood out amid the tattered volumes and porcelain figurines as if it were daubed with luminous paint. I reckoned that two steps would be enough for me to seize it.

I took a sip of coffee with exaggerated gusto, as if it was some potion that would give me the courage I needed. I rose from the sofa without any specific idea in mind but driven by the conviction that I must shake up this scene that threatened to perpetuate itself from one Sunday to the next, like a colored print from which we would disappear one by one, in age order or possibly at random, leaving a dramatic gap on the sofa like an extracted molar. I needed to find out who the letter belonged to, to confirm that at least one of my in-laws was a person of the world, full of emotional turmoil.

I stood in front of the shelf, pretending to read the titles, listening to Eva and her family chatting behind me. I noticed my hand quaking, my palm moist with sweat as, one by one, I began to run my fingers over the spines of the books—*El estudiante de Salamanca*, *El burlador de Sevilla*, poems by Federico García Lorca, a guide to the Thyssen museum, an essay on oncology—as I neared my objective. Were my in-laws following my movements? By the time my fingers paused at the battered volume by Tolstoy, my heart was in my throat. I plucked the book from the shelf with an excessively brusque gesture, like a would-be thief, and swung around, presenting the book to my audience as if it was all part of the same choreographed movement. "This is one of my favorite novels," I declared.

An awkward silence ensued. They turned to look at me as one, more startled by my raised voice than by my confession. My father-in-law glanced at the book in a dismissive way that was soon extended to me before he went back to watching the television. For her part, Angeline simply stared at it, as though unsure what I was holding. The person I least expected to respond exclaimed with girlish enthusiasm: "Oh, but that's *Anna Karenina!*" Eva rose from the sofa and came over to where I was standing, a look of bewilderment on my face. With a reverential gesture, she took the book from me, caressing its tattered cover as if it was a sparrow fallen from the nest. "This is my favorite book too," she said, "I used to read it every summer in the village. Do you remember, Mama? I even persuaded cousin Enrique to read it." Angeline nodded wistfully. *Enrique, her cousin from the village?* I thought to myself, increasingly alarmed. Had he written the letter? Eva continued to finger the cover, a blissful smile on her lips. I suspected she wasn't so much recalling passages from the book as her sexual encounters with her cousin, and I couldn't help thinking of him too: Queque, that burly, balding fellow, with his smiling red face, the owner of a company that sold GM foods, who would come for Christmas dinner each year bearing basketfuls of grotesque vegetables. And now that I thought about it, his whirlwind visits invariably left Eva with an air of melancholy. Didn't she appear distracted whenever she prepared a salad, mesmerized by those tomatoes the size of small boulders, those peppers with turned-up ends like Moorish slippers? And what about their behavior toward each other? More than once, I had felt a twinge of jealousy when I noticed their lingering embraces, or when I saw Enrique stroke her hair, or massage her shoulders while we were watching television, sharing an intimacy whose origins I only now understood. Had he not once called her "Karenina," smiling inscrutably while the rest of us raised our eyebrows? "If you like it so much, take it," Jacob said suddenly, his eyes still fixed on the screen. Eva appeared to consider the possibility for an instant. "No," she said at last, "I shan't be reading it again." And she returned it to the shelf with a solemn gesture, which to me seemed bristling with symbolic meaning.

Soon after, the Sunday visit came to an end. We pulled on our coats, said goodbye, and walked back to the car. I drove home, making no attempt to break Eva's silence, as she observed the streets with a placid smile etched on her lips. I knew we were both thinking about the same thing, although I was visualizing it while she was remembering it: a younger Eva, almost a girl, running her hands over her cousin's body. That body that, summer after summer, had turned into a David, slowly emerging from the marble's depths. That strong, youthful body, the closeness of which had begun to produce butterflies in her stomach. That smooth, supple body she threw her arms around in the pool as they tried to duck each other, the grown-ups laughing, oblivious to the desire fermenting between them—that dark fire that there was only one way to quench. I had no idea what might have gone on between them afterward, when that awkward game started to resemble love, forcing her cousin to write the letter I had read, although it wasn't difficult to imagine. Clearly, my wife hadn't gone to the rendezvous; or perhaps she had, but only to persuade her cousin, who was older than her, that this was a youthful whim. I don't know whether she succeeded or not, but obviously, as time went by, they had resigned themselves to building separate lives, perhaps with someone who resembled their first love, but without the impediment of being a blood relative. That was why, whenever they met, they looked at each other with the complicity of people who share a secret that is stronger than any bond they might establish with someone else. In a strange way, I envied them. I glanced at Eva, wondering whether I could go on living with her now that I knew her secret. *Who doesn't have secrets?* I thought to myself. I had to be the only person on the planet who didn't. In my life, there was nothing interesting to conceal, only monotony and vacuousness. It was then that I realized there was something far more terrible than having a secret: not having any. And so I took a symbolic deep breath and prepared to confront the rest of my life with Eva and her nice cousin Queque from the village. Queque, to whom, if at Christmas I saw him vanish with my wife only to reappear a few minutes later disheveled and euphoric, as if they had locked themselves in the bathroom for old times' sake, while my mother-in-law was slicing the turkey in the dining room, I might feel obliged to recommend a book chosen at random from the shelf.

"Alfred was a fan of Tolstoy too," Eva said suddenly, "although I never saw him read a book." She spoke with an air of surprise, as if she had glimpsed a strange coincidence in all this. Except I could imagine Alfred pacing around my in-laws' living room, randomly picking out Tolstoy's book, his eyes opening wide as he saw a small piece of yellowing paper fall at his feet.

Snow Globe

Alberto had not realized how much he longed to be held by someone until that strange old lady flung herself at him with the obvious intention of wrapping him in her arms. How long had it been since he had been able to indulge in such a gesture of affection? It was impossible at his workplace, and for a long time now his feelings for his father were reduced to the almost religious kiss he planted on his forehead every night. As for Cristina, tired of casual employment, she had decided to immerse herself in preparing for the civil service exams, so that their encounters were reduced to awkward exchanges on the gloomy landing of a rickety stairwell while her mother spied on them through a crack in the door, pretending to be busy in the kitchen. Hungry for human contact, Alberto returned the old lady's gesture without thinking, almost as a reflex: he folded his arms round her, careful not to crush her bones, which felt as fragile as a wafer, inhaling the smell of her wrinkled skin, and surrendering to the godsend of this unexpected contact. Methodical and appreciative, he held her firmly, replenishing himself as from a pitcher, aware that this couldn't last, and that soon the old lady would look him in the face and realize that the darkness of the corridor had led her to mistake the encyclopedia salesman for one of her nearest and dearest.

However, when at last they disentangled themselves and stood gazing at one another, the old lady's lips were curved in a broad smile.

"José Luis, my son," she exclaimed, her voice cracking with emotion. "I knew that you'd come, that you wouldn't forget your mother on her birthday."

Startled, Alberto blinked as he thought he detected the cloudiness of cataracts in the old lady's eyes. This, added to the dim light from the naked bulb in the corridor, would explain her mistake. He was about to correct her when the old lady began to propel him along the tomb-like passageway that gave way to a tiny room crammed with antique furniture, most of it buried beneath a litter of crocheted cloths. Lining the shelves were an array of tasteless ornaments and kitschy trinkets that seemed to have proliferated in the semidarkness of the room like nocturnal creatures. The only hint of color was a birthday cake bristling with candles on the table.

"Sit down, son, and let's cut the cake. You must be starving," the old lady said, handing him a paper hat, similar to the one she proceeded to place on her own gray locks.

Motionless in the center of the room, Alberto stared dumb-founded at the old lady as she sat expectantly at the table, her face softened by the glow from the candles, the tilt of her hat redeeming her frail figure. *Well, why not?* he thought to himself. He had spent all day traipsing around the outskirts of the city, his overcoat buttoned up to the neck, hunched ever lower against the icy winter wind that, if one was to heed those occasional premonitions brought on by rheuma-tism, indicated that snow was on the way for the first time in twelve years. Viewed from this perspective, the table beneath whose skirts a small heater must be alight seemed to him like a refuge, a mother's womb, a trench from which to listen in safety to the roar of shells. It cost him nothing to stand in for the ungrateful José Luis and offer his aging mother a few crumbs of happiness.

His mind made up, he set his briefcase down on the floor, took a seat in the rocking chair, and with the deliberate gestures of a practiced surgeon, picked up the cake knife. Emphasizing his assumed relaxed air by humming a tune, he cut the cake, all the while casting sidelong glances at the old lady, who in turn watched him with a contented smile. After serving, they each tucked into their slice amid a convent-like silence, broken only by the sighs of pleasure they gave in praise of the baker's expertise.

While they were devouring the confection, Alberto noticed two photographs hanging on one of the walls. One was of a dark-haired woman with pale skin and dreamy eyes, doubtless the old lady's daughter. The other was of a skinny individual with a plain face and aquiline nose, who must have been José Luis. Alberto had to admit there was a vague resemblance between him and the man he was substituting, although the person in the photograph had a determined look that he himself hadn't been lucky enough to be born with. Clearly José Luis belonged to that group of people who see life as an exciting challenge, and it wasn't hard to imagine him rushing about with rolled-up charts under his arm, or delving confidently into a surgery wearing latex gloves, or giving orders to a team of encyclopedia salesmen made up of those who had just enough blood in their veins to keep them alive. In any event, it was sad that he had something apparently more important to do than accompany his mother on her birthday. As sad as it was that he himself had nothing better to do somewhere else.

"Where's my present?" the old lady suddenly asked.

Her question startled Alberto. He peered at his hostess, not knowing what to say, until he remembered the gift he had bought for Cristina that very afternoon while wandering around a shopping center. He had gone this far, why not go the whole hog? he thought, fumbling in his case. He took out the gift, unwrapped it, and showed it to the old lady. She looked skeptically at the glass sphere sitting in Alberto's cupped hand.

"It's a snow globe," he explained.

He gave it a brusque shake, and snow instantly began to fall on the quaint little village enclosed inside. The old lady's face lit up when she saw the snowflakes appear as if from nowhere. She took it from Alberto with awe and, after a brief hesitation, ventured to shake it herself, conjuring once more the snow that fell on the miniature scene. Then, putting it to one side, as though wishing to save the pleasure for when she was alone, she smiled contentedly at her bogus son.

"It's a toy world that obeys its own laws," said Alberto, raising his eyebrows toward the globe. "Everything inside it works differently."

The old lady nodded gravely, although she couldn't possibly have understood what he was talking about. Alberto immediately chided himself for having responded to the old lady's kindly disposition with his impressions of the snow globe in the form of that private, stupid thought, but it was too late. Then he recalled how he'd ventured into that store in the shopping center for no other reason than to muster the courage to go back outside to face the cold. He had wandered around the aisles, looking at the cheap trinkets as a feeling of hopelessness crept up on him. Would he fritter away the future with this same feeling of apathy, wasting his time hanging around in bars and stores like a beggar who doesn't even have the solace of wine to disguise his useless existence? What was he supposed to do if he wasn't even strong enough to face the elements, and couldn't even find a dream to pursue, a desire he could devote himself to attaining, if only to show some mettle? Sometimes he would examine his life, weighing and measuring his day, and find only a small change: the rush of pleasure when he sold an encyclopedia, the triumph of stealing a kiss or caress from Cristina—scant gratification for his perseverance in the landing's silent gloom—and he would go to bed defeated, terrified at the prospect that this world was immutable, that for things to change he would need willpower. Lost in these morbid thoughts, his eyes had fallen upon the snow globe standing on a shelf. Inside it, the maker had enclosed a fairy-tale village, made up of four or five log cabins and a few fir trees. Without knowing why, Alberto imagined he was living in one of the cabins in the globe, surrounded by neighbors who, like him, had abandoned a hostile existence, and who were determined to make this imaginary life work. Finally, compelled by the shop assistant's increasingly suspicious looks, he had purchased the snow globe, that world within a world, subject to the laws of a god who only had the power to sprinkle them with a bit of harmless snow from time to time.

"Your sister should be calling soon," the old lady suddenly declared, waking Alberto from his reverie. Thrown for an instant, Alberto fixed his eyes on the photograph of the woman on the wall, not without a measure of alarm. "She never used to call, you know. But since the day I took her to task, she hasn't forgotten once."

At that moment, as if the old lady's words were a spell, the phone rang. Alberto started and glanced about for the device making that harsh, impertinent noise. He discovered it on a nearby side table, hidden under a pile of junk. The old woman rose laboriously, went over to the apparatus, and picked up the receiver.

"Hello, my dear," she said, visibly moved. "How are you? Is it cold in Brussels?"

Touched, Alberto watched the old lady as she stood next to the table swaying lightly as if the weight of the earpiece was upsetting her balance. As he listened to her talking, he admired her wizened frame, the accumulation of years that lay before him, and he couldn't help feeling slightly dizzy as he became conscious that the old lady had lived in a different time from him, that she had been alive when he was nothing more than a remote possibility, a hypothesis made reality by the stubbornness of a cobbler who wouldn't give up until the daughter of his best customer agreed to accompany him to the Christmas dance. He observed the forlorn creature with infinite tenderness, marveling at all the experiences her eyes must have stored up and regretting it was a legacy that had no heir, one that would be washed down the drain when death finally decided to pull the plug on her. What kind of life had fate allotted her? he wondered. Judging from the lowly hovel where she spent her days, she must have led the thankless and anonymous life of a worker bee, the kind that always seems to take place alongside real life, whatever that might be. Together with a husband, who doubtless had died a few years ago and about whom Alberto could fathom nothing, the woman had courageously raised two children, for whom no sacrifice was too great, and now she doubtless considered the few years she had left as idle time, which she had no idea how to employ. At that point in life, thought

Alberto, having fulfilled all our duties, all we can do is sit down and preserve our energy, enjoy the love of our nearest and dearest and the satisfaction of knowing that we are the hidden creators of their achievements, that we have brought into the world someone who by their actions shows us our efforts were worthwhile. Although it was obvious that her children had denied her the pleasure of seeing them build their lives. At any rate, the daughter was calling from far-off Brussels. This fellow José Luis, who apparently had remained in the city, couldn't even be bothered to do that. Saddened, Alberto carried on eating his piece of cake as he listened to their conversation, slightly concerned where it might lead. He became alarmed when, after a few minutes of simply nodding at the chatter coming from the other end of the telephone, the old lady said:

"You needn't worry about me, my dear. I'm not alone. Your brother has come to see me."

Rigid in his chair, waiting to see what would happen next, Alberto slowly chewed the sugary morsel he had just put in his mouth. He heard the woman at the other end of the line say something in reply in a tone that sounded suddenly harsh, which left the old lady speechless for a moment, as if she was searching for the right response.

"Don't start that again, my dear," he heard her say. "Why do you always say the same thing? José Luis isn't dead! He didn't die in a plane crash! He's right here beside me, eating my birthday cake."

Alberto stopped chewing and fixed his gaze on the photograph of José Luis. Was he supplanting a dead man? He
glanced again at the old lady, who was still insisting that her
son was alive. But the other woman's voice made it plain she
wasn't about to give in.

"Come on, talk to your sister," the old lady suddenly ordered,
holding out the receiver. "Show her how dead you are."

Alberto looked at the telephone as if it were a snake. Not
knowing how to refuse without arousing his hostess's suspicions, he stood up and walked rather unsteadily over to the
phone. He seized the receiver, not knowing what to do.

"Hello, sister," he said, his heart pounding in his chest.
"How's everything?"

A sepulchral silence followed at the far end of the line.

"Who the hell are you, you son of a bitch?" he heard the
woman ask, once she had recovered from her surprise.

Despite the harshness of her tone, Alberto thought she had
a pleasant voice. He looked at her portrait on the wall, which
allayed his concern to some extent, as if knowing what she
looked like gave him some kind of strange advantage over her.
His silence provoked a barrage of insults and even a threat to
call the police if he didn't tell her who he was.

"Listen," said Alberto, lowering his voice, after making
sure that the old lady had returned to her chair and was no
longer within earshot, "I'm a simple encyclopedia salesman.
Your mother mistook me for your brother, and I decided to
play along. I don't mean her any harm, I assure you, and I'm

not going to rob her. I'm simply offering her some company, that's all. I'll finish my cake and then leave."

The woman remained silent for a few moments, taking in his explanation, while Alberto, aware of how bizarre the truth sounded, feared she might not believe him. But to his astonishment, when the unfamiliar voice spoke again it was to apologize and thank him for what he was doing for her mother.

"She's very lonely, the poor thing," the woman explained in a gentle, slow voice, as if she was thinking things over at the same time. "She hasn't been the same since José Luis died, you know? She refuses to accept that he's gone. She's constructed a world where everything is exactly as it was. Thank you for helping to make it more real. That's what we all do."

Not daring to interrupt, Alberto let her continue, aware that the woman was simply unburdening herself. When she fell silent again, he insisted that she had no reason to thank him: the cake was delicious, and he'd had nothing better to do that evening. The woman gave a little laugh, which sounded extraordinarily sweet to Alberto's ears. It seemed incongruous to hear such a delicate, diaphanous sound in that bleak room sunk in the clammy despair of sorrows, and he was on the verge of asking her if she could laugh again, if she could caress his eardrums with that flutter of light, but this felt like too bold and unseemly a request between two strangers. Uncomfortable in the silence that settled over them once everything had been explained, they said a hasty goodbye.

As he hung up, Alberto was surprised to realize that in far-off Brussels a woman he didn't know was imitating his gesture. He had guessed from the old lady's comments that the woman wasn't married and didn't appear to be living with anyone, and so he imagined her sitting on a sofa, dressed in a simple pair of striped pajamas, the type usually worn by men, her dark hair wet and shiny after the shower she treated herself to as a fitting end to the wearisome day in some government office, between whose walls her life was draining away without her noticing. He placed her in a small apartment, tastefully decorated if without much flair, possibly overlooking a small park carpeted with fallen leaves that crunched almost melodiously as she walked through it in the mournful twilight every evening. He had no idea how much of what he had just imagined was true. Possibly he was only right about the sofa or the pajamas. But what he could be certain of was that at that very moment the woman was thinking about him. She might never do so again, but just then she was conjuring him up, endowing him with a body, compelled by that reflex action that moves us to give a face to strangers who call us on the telephone. And the fact that, even though they'd never met or seen each other before, they were thinking about each other in perfect unison, separated by an ocean of miles, gave him a pleasant sensation of complicity.

Alberto noticed that the old lady had dozed off. *Too much excitement for one day*, he thought. He took off his paper hat, left it on the table, and, after retrieving his briefcase, smiled a goodbye at her. He closed the door to the apartment quietly and descended the stairs. In the hallway, he paused to glance at the mailboxes, feeling a need to give his hostess a name. He found the corresponding box and ran his finger over the little plaque, touching the letters that made up the old lady's identity the way a blind person might do.

"It's her birthday today," a voice behind him said.

Startled, Alberto wheeled round. The ground-floor neighbor, a woman of about sixty, was watching him from the half-open door to her apartment, holding a plate wrapped in tinfoil.

"Doña Elvira, that is. It's her birthday today. I'm just going to take her some donuts I made. The poor thing is very lonely. Do you know her?"

"A little," replied Alberto, uneasy at being interrogated by the woman. She was eyeing him suspiciously, the plate wobbling perilously. "I was a friend of José Luis," he felt obliged to add, hoping that might reassure her.

"He was a wonderful boy," the woman said, seemingly pleased to meet one of the dead man's friends. "Losing him was a terrible blow for Elvira. The truth is, I don't know how she's able to bear it. Especially since, two months after the accident, José Luis's sister, who blamed herself for his death, took her own life by swallowing a bottle of pills."

Alberto felt unable to breathe. His head started to spin and, fearing he might faint, he said goodbye to the neighbor with an unintelligible murmur and made a dash for the front door. The freezing night air helped him to recover his composure. He leaned against a lamppost, gasping for breath. The daughter had died as well? Then who had he been talking to? he wondered, as he felt a shiver go down his spine. Had he just spoken with a ghost? Recalling the woman's voice, her tinkling laugh, he felt afraid, a terrible, exaggerated fear, and at the same time he felt something like a profound revulsion as he realized that he had been in touch with someone who didn't exist, with someone who lived in another world. But that was impossible, he told himself, desperately searching for some alternative explanation as panic engulfed him. It was more logical to suppose that he hadn't been talking to the woman in the photograph but to someone else, possibly her roommate, who like him had pretended to be a dead person. Perhaps the old lady, sunk in her loneliness and mad with grief after her daughter's death, continued to dial the number at her apartment each night to scold her for never calling, and her ex-roommate, taking pity on her, had decided to supplant her friend. That idea, which was far more sensible, calmed him.

Feeling reassured, he buttoned up his coat and promised himself he would continue to play his role. He would return each year, put on the paper hat, cut the cake, wait for the call from that unknown woman, and talk to the sister he'd never had. It was perfectly possible that, even if his real life never went anywhere and remained stuck on the landing of the stairwell at Cristina's house, in this other life, the unknown woman would come to visit them, sit in the other empty rocking chair in the room, and while he listened to her talking about Brussels, he would be able to take her hand beneath the skirts of the table. And it wouldn't matter to him that it was as cold as his own must be, because why should he care if she had died after swallowing a bottle of pills and him in a plane crash if the three of them were now together in a world of lies, a world within a world where they could be happy. He smiled as snowflakes started to fall from the sky in slow, gentle drifts, as if someone somewhere had shaken a snow globe.

The Land of the Dolls

At that time of evening, the playground resembled a child-hood graveyard. The swings creaked mournfully in the breeze, the slide rose toward the moon like an absurd, useless object, and the crisscrossed bars of the climbing frame traced the skeleton of an impossible dinosaur . . . Without the clamor of children, without their shouting and running, the enclosure might have been mistaken for one of those apocalyptic film landscapes, where life has been systematically wiped out by some mysterious virus—if it wasn't for me, that is, circling the playground apparatus with a melancholy air. I had gone back to search for Jasmyn, my daughter's doll, though even before I arrived I knew that I wouldn't find her. We don't live in the calm, rational universe where forgotten dolls remain where we left them, but in the neighboring universe, that cruel domain governed by wars, brutality, and uncertainty, where orphaned objects instantly disappear, possibly because, unbeknownst to us, the things we forget go to make up the dowry we will possess in that other world.

I have to confess that finding Jasmyn would have restored my self-confidence. She was an ordinary plastic doll, skinny, with a slightly oversized head, like all dolls nowadays, and came already baptized from the factory. My daughter had endowed her with a degree of humanity and took her everywhere, as if she were the little sister Nuria and I had refused to give her. Ever since we had presented our daughter with the doll the previous Christmas, we had been forced to get used to this diminutive woman occupying a place at the table, in the car, on the sofa. We had no idea whether this was a reminder of our failure to continue to procreate or simply because Laura could no longer be without her passive companion.

Though I was tempted to take advantage of Laura's carelessness to rid us of the doll's irksome presence, I was painfully aware that in the previous few months my image as a father had suffered a progressive decline, and it occurred to me that arriving home with the doll in my arms would redeem me in my daughter's eyes, and possibly also in those of my wife. However, after combing the playground several times, I realized forlornly that this was just another pipe dream, yet another impossible enterprise, and that I would once again discover my natural incapacity to deal with the problems of life under Nuria's scornful gaze.

The prospect of returning home without the doll was not a pleasant one, and I found myself loitering, even though I knew my wife was going out that evening to one of those inconvenient work dinners that were so flagrantly encroaching on our love life—the only area of our marriage that was still free from recriminations. I imagine it was my eagerness to postpone the inevitable that led me to enter the café near my house when I saw my colleague Víctor Cordero inside.

Víctor taught literature at the same secondary school as me, and although I had never warmed to his verbose, rather presumptuous nature, the shared workplace had made our relations friendly enough. It was scarcely a year since I had arranged regular dinners with Víctor and his wife with the purpose of injecting new life into my marriage. These were forced affairs, which I struggled to keep going for four or five months, until I became weary of the insufferable banter he and Nuria couldn't help engaging in over the grilled turbot and vegetables. When Víctor and his wife separated, and he returned to a bachelor's predatory habits and lewd jokes, I finally threw in the towel, and the dinners died a natural death, like wilted roses that have fulfilled their mission of beauty.

"What are you doing in my territory, stranger?" I said, cocking my forefinger at him. "Don't you know this here neighborhood isn't big enough for both of us?"

Víctor seemed surprised to see me, but quickly composed himself, grinning smugly.

"I'm enjoying the benefits of being single, Diego," he replied, inviting me to sit with him. "Now that no one is waiting at home for me, I'm free to explore the city at my leisure. I'm the fuckin' Lone Ranger, my friend."

"Right," I replied skeptically.

Víctor had always struck me as someone incapable of being alone, because of his incessant need to see himself favorably reflected in other peoples' eyes.

Taking the brandy glass he held out to me, I added, almost in a whisper, "I couldn't live without Nuria."

"What's your excuse?" Victor said at last. "Why are you out so late?"

I was preparing to think up some pretext when, to my surprise, I found myself telling him the truth. Possibly it was the comforting sensation of the brandy trickling down my throat, or the dense silence enveloping the streets, or the exquisite display of stars the sky had put on for nobody in particular, or possibly a conspiracy of all of the above, that made me consider this man, with whom I had no affinity, the ideal custodian of my cares. I told him about the doll, embellishing my story with my existential anguish and the complexities of my frustrations as a father, as you might send a written complaint in the hope that someone higher up will listen and take pity on you. Once I had finished, Víctor gave a smirk, as if the real difficulty was my inability to solve problems, rather than the problem itself.

"You know what you could do," he said. I gazed at him in astonishment. The last thing I expected was for Víctor to come up with a solution, or even bother to try. "The same as

Kafka." I looked at him, puzzled. "You know, Franz Kafka, the Czech author?"

"Just because I teach math, Víctor, it doesn't mean I've never heard of Kafka." Víctor chuckled, and I realized from the way he sat upright in his chair, that he was going to subject me to another of his long-winded anecdotes about authors.

"Listen carefully," he said. "During the autumn of 1923, Kafka was accustomed to strolling in a park near his home in Berlin. He had moved there with Dora Diamant to spend what he thought were his last days. One afternoon, he came across a little girl who was crying her eyes out. He must have been intrigued enough by her grief to overcome his habitual shyness, and he asked her what was the matter. The little girl replied that she had lost her doll. Just like your daughter, Diego. And what did the author do? Moved by her plight, he promptly disguised the sad truth the best way he knew how: through fiction. 'Your doll has gone away on a trip,' he assured her. The girl stopped crying and eyed Kafka suspiciously. 'How do you know?' she asked. 'Because she sent me a letter,' he improvised. 'I don't have it with me now,' he said sorrowfully, 'but I'll bring it for you tomorrow.' The girl seemed unimpressed, but agreed to return the next day. That night, one of the greatest authors in the world shut himself away in his study to write a story directed at a single reader. And, according to Dora Diamant, he did so with the same seriousness and intensity he applied to all his works. In that first letter, the doll explained that although she greatly enjoyed the little girl's company, she needed a change of scene, to see the world. She promised she would write to her every day to keep her informed of her adventures. And so it was that Kafka composed a letter every night for the last three weeks of his life," Víctor said reverentially. "A magnificent personal remedy designed to cure the sorrows of an unknown child. This was Kafka's last work. You could say that he wrote it with his dying breath." My colleague shook his head mournfully. "Alas, the letters were lost," he murmured.

Speechless, I sipped my brandy. Did Víctor seriously imagine that I, who had never written a word in my life, could resort to such a convoluted ploy to console my daughter? Or had he simply used the opportunity of our chance encounter to dredge up another of the weird anecdotes he collected like rare orchids?

Back home, I pondered the matter. Undoubtedly, it was a charming tale, but I wasn't Kafka, I was an ordinary math teacher, incapable of such flights of fancy. Wouldn't it be easier to buy my daughter an identical doll? The fact is, I returned home that evening defeated yet again, except that this time, from the angry look Nuria gave me as she breezed past on her way out to her work dinner, I had taken even longer than the prescribed period to demonstrate my ineptitude. I sighed despairingly as my wife left, slamming the door behind her. However, the worst was yet to come, I told myself, noticing the light coming from Laura's bedroom door, which was ajar. My daughter was awake, waiting for Jasmyn.

I approached her room with the resignation of a prisoner on his way to the gallows. I didn't have to say a word, Laura burst into tears as soon as she saw I was empty-handed. I sat down beside her and put my arms around her. It was then, as I cradled her, trembling in my arms, that I resolved to become a different man. I wasn't going to give in this time; I was going to act. I was going to surprise everyone. How could I not do something for my own daughter that the Czechoslovakian author had done for a little girl he didn't even know?

When Laura fell asleep, I prepared a flask of coffee and shut myself in my study. I had no idea what would come of all this, quite possibly nothing, and yet I refused to let that deter me. I wanted to comfort my daughter, and this very unique method was as good as any other. I started off by disguising my writing, which I made smaller and flatter, until it looked conceivably as if it could have been penned by Jasmyn's tiny, plastic hand. That was the easiest part. Composing the letter in which Jasmyn explained to my daughter the reasons for her sudden disappearance took me most of the night. By the time Nuria came home, I was still holed up in my study trying to think like a doll. I wasn't too convinced by the final result. Even so, I placed it in an envelope and, over breakfast the next day, I plucked it from my jacket pocket and waved it in front of Laura's tearstained face.

"Look what someone pushed under the door this morning: a letter from Jasmyn." While Nuria eyed me over the rim of her coffee cup with her usual disdain, Laura seized the letter with a mixture of suspicion and interest. She tore open the envelope and started to read. My pulse quickened as her eyes widened as they slid along the delicate lines traced on the paper. Slowly, her face started to light up, as Jasmyn told Laura that she loved her deeply, but that sooner or later all curious dolls like her had to set off on a journey to the mythical Land of the Dolls, a land inhabited by others like her, toys that had chosen to live without children, to pursue their own lives, far away from everything that reminded them of their sad condition as playthings. Jasmyn wasn't sure that this place existed. Maybe it was a fantasy world, a myth propagated by dolls in shop windows to make their incarceration more bearable. And yet, she felt duty bound to embark on this journey into the unknown, in the hope that she might one day find herself there. Laura's lips parted in a smile when Jasmyn assured her that she, Laura, would be welcome in this Land of the Dolls, and even offered to send a map with directions on how to get there, assuming it really existed and she succeeded in finding it.

From that day on, I followed Kafka's example and shut myself away in my study to devise those letters, which, like a playful child, I would push under the front door every morning. Laura soon came to expect them and would get up before the alarm clock went off, just like on Christmas Eve, eager to discover how far Jasmyn had gotten in her search for the Land of the Dolls. Seeing her curled up in an armchair in the living room hunched over my letters, I felt a surge of pride. Not just because it proved to me that this time I had found the correct solution to the problem, but because the eagerness with which she devoured my words suggested I had done a more than satisfactory job. Moreover, my daughter never told us what was in the letters, as if that was a secret between her and her doll, thus imbuing my humble flights of fancy with even greater meaning.

I had hoped that Nuria might appreciate the considerable effort I was making to alleviate our child's suffering, or at least admire the inspired strategy I had devised—given that I decided not to tell her I had lifted the idea from an author called Franz Kafka who had lived in the last century. Apart from anything else, I doubted she had ever heard of him, as reading didn't play a big part in Nuria's life, apart from gossip magazines, home and garden supplements, and supermarket catalogues. And yet, every morning, Nuria would observe my bizarre antics with a look of indifference. She saw me slide the envelope under the door, then hurry back to my chair in the dining room, as though witnessing the behavior of a complete lunatic. Perhaps she thought Laura should know the truth, and that all this was going to affect her mind, turning her into a hopeless dreamer, incapable of living in the adult world, where there was no room for fantasy, but I doubted that. I suspected her cool response had more to do with the fact that we had reached the point of no return and that no matter what I did, whether I saved a child from a burning building or was nominated for the Nobel Prize, she couldn't admire me. The resentment she had built up toward me over the years made that impossible. The days when we dazzled each other were long gone. We now found ourselves trapped in a quagmire into which we were slowly sinking, together and yet unable to hold hands, since apparently we even rejected the affection we had once felt for each other, now seeing it as some kind of infectious disease. A quagmire upon which we had built a refuge against the world, a refuge that turned out to be as fragile as a house of cards.

And yet, this hardly mattered to me, because I had discovered a far more comforting refuge in Jasmyn's letters. At last, I had discovered something I was really good at, which gave meaning to my otherwise meaningless life. And so, while my marriage quietly fell apart and I drank of the bitter cup of sorrow, Jasmyn experienced happiness. Because, if no one appeared to be looking out for us in the universe we inhabited, in the pocket-sized world created by my pen, I was a watchful, benevolent God, who could clear the path of Jasmyn's destiny of all obstacles, without her having to kneel and beg me for it in any church. My hand was responsible for Jasmyn traveling all over Europe, staying in boxes belonging to toys she met along the way as if they were safe houses, while she drew ever closer to her longed-for Land of the Dolls. After consulting the atlas, I decided to locate it in the Himalayas, in a small valley at the foot of Mount Everest, where all the dolls lived in peace and harmony, tilling the land by day and singing songs around bonfires at night. Jasmyn now wrote her letters by the light of those fires. She said how much she missed Laura and that one night, although she had not been designed for this in the factory, she had shed real tears as she looked at a photograph of Laura she had stolen from our family album before she left, which I kept hidden in my wallet. By this time, little Laura was cured, and so I decided it was time for Jasmyn to confess that she couldn't send her a map that would guide her to the Land of the Dolls, as everyone there had taken a silent vow to protect their world. Jasmyn also confessed that she had fallen in love with Crown, a warrior doll who wore a sword at his belt, black velvet boots, and had been appointed Captain of the Guard, whose job it was to defend the kingdom.

The day when news of Jasmyn's wedding arrived was the day Nuria decided to leave me. There was no point in going on, she said, as she lugged her suitcase toward the front door. Although I'd been expecting it, the fact that she chose to abandon me at the exact moment when I was being such an excellent father was extremely painful. Inspired by something akin to professional pride, and in the vain hope of eliciting her praise, I couldn't help referring smugly to my most recent endeavors. Nuria shook her head to emphasize her disappointment.

"You should be doing other things than filling our daughter's head with nonsense," she said disdainfully. "You aren't Kafka, Diego."

I was so astonished at having been exposed in this way that I didn't know what to say. And when one doesn't know what to say, it is invariably the voice of despair that speaks.

"I can't live without you, Nuria," I murmured. This naive, schoolboy admission hung in the air, neither of us knowing what to do with it.

"Goodbye, Diego," Nuria said finally, closing the door behind her.

Dazed, I stood in the hallway for a few minutes trying to think of what to do. I would wait an hour, and then call Nuria's sister's place, where I assumed my wife had gone, and do my utmost to convince her to come back. But first, I had to console my daughter, to whom Nuria had been talking before she left, shut away in her bedroom.

Laura was sitting on her bed, staring blankly at the wall. I sat down beside her and tried to find a way to explain the situation. I was about to speak, when she placed her hand on mine.

"Don't worry, Dad," she said, her eyes still fixed on the wall. "Mom will come back. I know she will."

This made me choke back my words, as my eyes filled with tears. Our world was collapsing around us, but for the moment it was best to ignore the sound of cascading rubble. This was what my daughter was suggesting. We sat side by side for a while, plunged in a cathedral-like silence, until my daughter fell asleep on the bed, and I drew the covers over her, feeling that she should be drawing them over me.

It was then, stroking my daughter's hair as night descended over the city, that I remembered something from my conversation with Nuria that I had overlooked at the time: How did she know that I'd employed the same strategy with Laura that Franz Kafka had used almost a century earlier on the little girl in the park?

I leaped to my feet, overwhelmed by a certainty I refused to believe even though everything seemed to point to it being true. I stumbled along the corridor, the pieces of a puzzle that had been there all the time falling into place in my mind. Confirming my theory was terribly simple. I only had to park my car opposite Víctor's apartment and go up there when I saw him leave for work. I rang the bell, knowing who would open the door.

"You can't live without me," I said before her horrified gaze.

I arrived back home just in time to take Laura to school. As I went up in the elevator, it occurred to me that this was the first time in a month that no letter would be waiting for her when she got up, and so I was surprised when my foot touched an envelope as I opened the door. I picked it up off the floor, scarcely able to believe my eyes. But the letter wasn't from Jasmyn. It was from Nuria, addressed to me. In it she assured me this wasn't goodbye, that she would be back, but first she needed to see the world, to find herself. Her words might have given me enormous consolation, had they not been printed in the clumsy, strained handwriting of my nine-year-old daughter.

Laura and I exchanged glances before dissolving in a tearful embrace. I realized that my daughter had always known, but had preferred to believe the beautiful lie I had invented, rather than imagine her doll broken, possibly thrown into a ditch. And now she was offering me the chance to believe that mine would come back too, even though I couldn't help remembering her body sprawled across Víctor's bed, the marks of my fingers around her throat, and a last look of reproach in her eyes, because she didn't approve of my way of handling that situation either.

A Fairy-Tale Life

"We are stories telling stories, nothing."

—Ricardo Reis

Once upon a time, there was an office worker by the name of Pelayo Díaz. One afternoon in mid-December, he was contemplating the Christmas gift basket on his table with such intense, extravagant hatred it was as if he thought it might get up and walk away at any moment. The gift basket was as ordinary as could be: Christmas cake rings, coconut balls, cans of peaches and pineapple in syrup, a couple of bottles of *cava*, several bars of *turrón*, all wrapped in a mosquito net of green cellophane and topped off with a complicated red bow. It contained nothing different from the previous year's or anything that led it to deserve such an exaggerated scrutiny. But Pelayo knew himself well enough to be aware that thanks to this kind gesture, the insurance company he worked for was inevitably condemning him to an interminable week of stomachaches: he belonged to that category of manic, obsessive people who are experts at transforming the most trivial event into a tragedy. *Never leave until tomorrow what could be done today* was one of the maxims he was inexorably governed by.

Pelayo remembered with a shudder how receiving this gift from his firm had filled him with hope the previous year. Their recognition meant a lot to him. After two long years working in the streets, he'd celebrated with sugar-coated fruits the fact that now he had a desk job in a heated office. In those days, the only Christmas present he'd received was a card so impersonal that even the frolicking of the shepherds around their bonfire seemed fake. Happy to belong to the big family of a company where it was not completely impossible he might get ahead, that night Pelayo had pulled a bar of *turrón* out of the gift basket and shoved the rest into the fridge. Little did he realize that this gesture would mark the beginning of a nightmarish episode that ended with him being admitted to the hospital.

Later on, Pelayo raided his fridge in search of the can of peaches. After a series of anxious calculations, he realized that if he ate at his usual speed he would not be able to finish the whole basket without some of it going bad. The next day, he turned up at the office with his belt let out another notch, a dead weight in his stomach, and the taste of honey on his tongue, which made him want to retch when he saw the romantic novels the gleeful receptionists were reading to pass the time between phone calls. Despite the protests from his stomach advising him against any further indulgence, Pelayo was unable to sit at his computer and see anything but rotting fruit on the screen. When he returned home that evening, he tried to carry on as normal, but found it impossible to concentrate on anything without having to make regular visits to the fridge to check that it was still plugged in, that it was the same docile domestic appliance as ever, incapable of betrayal of any kind. It was then that he understood he had been offered a poisoned chalice. He realized there was only one way to put an end to this dreadful situation: to eliminate the root cause of the problem. Still imprinted on Pelayo's memory were the furious swaying of an ambulance, the unpleasant familiarity with which the oxygen mask fitted on his face, the tube pushing gaily up his nostril and then snaking down inside him, and above all the disgusting suction that led him to realize that however many jails he might find himself in, he would never suffer any greater violation.

This time, when the firm's delivery boy arrived at his apartment with this year's Christmas gift basket, Pelayo Díaz felt so dizzy he almost collapsed onto the carpet. It was like a fresh encounter with a past enemy he had thought was dead. He watched, horrified, as the messenger laid it down on the living room table, astonished he even had the nerve to stretch out a hand in the hope of being rewarded for having brought this spawn of Satan into his house. Pelayo quickly got rid of him with a few coins bathed in the glittering sweat from his palm, shut the door on him, and turned to look at the accursed gift basket staring at him with a haughty, challenging air from his living room table. He knew he had lost from the start, aware that he did not have the courage simply to throw it away in the dumpster around the corner, from which countless babies were recovered every day. He tried to steel himself to face an existence of years crowned by the continual reappearance of the gift basket, which would remind him with blameless punctuality that hell reeked of molasses. Overwhelmed, he collapsed on the sofa, building up his strength to face his sickly destiny, trying to convince himself that the nurse who had attended him last time had been thinner than he remembered, and that the fact that she had plunged a tube in his throat implied an intimacy that just needed to be nurtured.

It was at this point that he considered the possibility of giving the gift basket away. An image came into his mind of that little old grandma he had met the year before, when he was pounding the streets in search of clients he could swindle in order to earn his miserable commission. That afternoon, he had been combing a neighborhood on the outskirts without much hope. The fact that this old woman had opened the door to him so readily, without rejecting him through the peephole or subjecting him to a police interrogation with the chain on, had stayed with him. Not to mention the evident poverty that Pelayo was able to glimpse over her shoulder, which had encouraged him to excuse himself and say goodbye, determined to leave the same way he had arrived—without a commission, but keeping his scruples intact. To swindle an old lady whom life already appeared to have relentlessly cheated seemed to him an unworthy act.

And then she seized him by the arm, in an almost despairing gesture, and invited him in. She could put some coffee on, and there must still be some buns from the last time she had a visitor. Wasting half an hour keeping a lonely, so obviously poor, old woman company, having to listen to her tell him about how her children had abandoned her, or about all her aches and pains, did not seem like a rewarding enterprise, whichever way he looked at it. Even to this day, Pelayo finds it hard to explain why he accepted her invitation. The fact is that no sooner had he nodded his head than this skinny old lady, wearing a housecoat that must once have been blue and smelled of mint candies, was already pushing him down a hallway as gloomy as a catacomb that led to a tiny, dark room so crammed with prehistoric pieces of furniture that it looked like an antique shop. Pelayo understood immediately that this must be her lair, because the air was filled with the smell of mint in a way that could only be explained by the constant, uninterrupted chewing of industrial quantities of soothing sweets. The room was so cramped that the bits of furniture seemed to rub up against one another like cattle in a barn. A narrow window let in a feeble light that settled on them like sawdust, so that Pelayo had to make a great effort to distinguish between a chest of drawers, a coat stand, a round table, twin rocking chairs, three smaller chairs, and what was possibly a bookcase, although he could not swear to it.

His hostess went off to make the coffee, and Pelayo was left sufficiently on his own to be able to go over to the row of portraits growing like muddy lichen on top of the chest of drawers. They were all the same person, displayed in chronological order, so that from left to right he could see how a little girl gradually grew into a woman. The old lady also appeared in some of them, always discreetly in the background, but as the photos progressed toward the right her presence became vaguer, as if she was starting to be superfluous. Pelayo could imagine how much it must hurt the old woman to glance at those images that only served to illustrate the way her solitude had gradually built up. He felt an intense dislike of the ungrateful girl smiling without remorse in the final photo, already enjoying her escape from the nest, the exciting adventure of independence. His hostess, after returning from the kitchen carrying a small tray on which a couple of coffee cups and a tin sugar bowl slid, rummaged in a drawer until she rescued a little plate containing what appeared to be the remnants of some distant Christmas past. She gestured daintily toward her guest to invite him to sit in one of the rocking chairs. Her gentleness, the picturesque chignon her hair was done up in, the innocence of her smile, and that delicate way she had of looking at him, plus the hallucinatory smell of mint, combined to create in Pelayo a sense of well-being he had not felt for centuries. Everything was encouraging him to spill his heart out. He sat back in the chair like someone stretching out on a couch, and before he realized it, the story of his life came pouring out of him while she smiled indulgently. Pelayo was amazed that an existence such as his, so bereft of any defining moments, could be made to last two full hours in the retelling. By the time he finished talking, darkness had fallen outside, and the two of them could only make each other out thanks to the little light that the grandmother must have switched on at some point during his garbled confession. He said good-bye with a much lighter soul, but without daring to look the old lady in the face, for fear of seeing bitter disappointment there, because without meaning to, it had been him rather than her who had poured out his troubles in that shadowy, mint-scented room.

Pelayo still blushed whenever he recalled the way he had bombarded his hostess with an icy autopsy of his own exis-tence, ruthlessly pruned of everything unimportant, only to discover how little there was left—nothing more than a bare trunk of irrefutable loneliness. A loneliness that could only be overcome, he had admitted in a rush of unabashed sincerity, by the longed-for company of a woman whom he described in his own terms as loving and innocent and as keen as he was to have someone to share a bed with after an exhausting, dismal workday. A woman capable of showing him why he was born, of instilling in him a wild desire to live with just one look; a woman he thought he glimpsed every day on the bus, in the park surrounded by pigeons, in the library, absorbed in an atlas, and whom he sometimes clumsily accosted, only to discover that she wasn't the one who would thaw the ice from his days, because if she didn't have time for a coffee, then she was far less likely to have enough to dissipate his fears and scare away the monsters. On his way home, Pelayo had reflected on the extraordinary way that people opened their hearts to perfect strangers, relieved by the certainty that nothing he had said could be used against him. The old woman deserved praise for the way she had weathered the storm. He felt he was almost obliged to give her the gift basket.

The three long hours before nightfall finally convinced him. Besides, he no longer needed to walk there: he had a car now. He would resolve the matter in half an hour and then return to his tranquil existence without dangers or gift baskets. He picked up the gift and, since it looked like rain, decided to try out the red coat his mother had given him back in July, with her usual foresight.

It wasn't difficult to find his car in the street. He had bought it secondhand as soon as he was promoted, weary of having to traipse everywhere, and still could not avoid a stab of emotion whenever he saw it waiting for him like a faithful old dog in the same spot he had left it the day before, the hood covered in frost, the wheels pissed on, the roof decorated by pigeons. Today, some kid from the neighborhood had written on the grungy windshield to tell him in labored handwriting that he was screwing his mother. Shaking his head at the graffiti with a disgust that was more theatrical than sincere, Pelayo climbed into the car, deposited the gift basket on the front passenger seat, and switched on the engine. The vehicle gave an anguished wheeze that boded ill, then fell silent, like a wounded animal that a coup de grace spares the cavalry of suffering. At this point, Pelayo discovered that his quota of hope was way above average, because he spent almost an hour repeating the gesture before admitting that the frozen battery had no intention whatsoever of producing the reviving spark that evening.

Depressed, he slumped back in his seat and stared forlornly at the gift basket. He contemplated going back up to his apartment and resigning himself then and there to the task of devouring its contents, but an image suddenly came into his mind of the pitiful old lady in her miserable little room, deprived of any kind of Christmas, drawing a creaking tune from the rocking chair with the slight bundle of her mint-intoxicated body. It was a shame that his good intentions would come to nothing, but it wasn't his fault that the car had chosen that very moment for its first act of betrayal. And yet, however many excuses Pelayo found to assuage his conscience, the Christmas gift basket seemed to be on a sacred mission to burst into that house on the outskirts and exorcise the spirit of Christmases without cheer.

Pelayo got out of the car, picked up the gift basket, and contemplated the far end of the street with a mixture of resignation and heroism, its horizon bristling with tall buildings enveloped in the play of light and dark brought on by the first storm clouds, the challenging gauntlet of this misty suburb that this evening seemed to have taken on a new mystery.

He strode off, not wishing to nitpick his memory in case the fact that he had only a vague recollection of where the old woman lived might end up completely undermining the faint hopes he still had for his mission. And yet, a long hour later he came to a halt, his hands frozen and his feet on fire, at a crossroads that completely punctured what remaining faith he had of being able to find her home. He remembered that the name of her street was Rosaleda, and he was almost sure he would recognize the building if he saw it, but this unexpected ramification of paths to follow only complicated matters further. Why was everything so difficult, why was the world organized so as to make even the most altruistic deed so awkward, why did living seem such a strenuous, painful effort? Annoyed, he looked up at the sky, only to see two dark clouds locking horns like bison. Up there, a storm was slowly building. The pub he saw on one of the street corners seemed to him the perfect place to recuperate, lift his spirits, and supply himself with inner warmth thanks to a glass of brandy.

He went into the bar, as long and thin as a freight train, and chose the table closest to the front window, from where he could observe both the comings and goings of passersby and the gathering clouds. Was it going to rain or not? Was all this suspense necessary? He ordered a brandy from a waiter who dragged himself over like a dying man, and after setting his soul on fire with a greedy gulp of the liquid, collapsed back in his seat and glanced angrily at the gift basket. Maybe it would be best to leave it there as if he had forgotten it, go home, decorate the tree, and put himself through the umpteenth rerun of *It's a Wonderful Life*, secure in the knowledge that life is sad, exhausting, disappointing—anything but beautiful.

Unable to make up his mind, Pelayo examined the pub around him. The clientele invariably depressed him because they were always such kindred spirits and rarely offered anything beyond a display of all the different varieties of loneliness that man can endure on his trip to oblivion. Scattered among the tables, drinks in hand, he could see people of every walk of life united by the trademark look of gazing into the middle distance; people who would possibly kill to escape from what, two tables away, another person would kill to have. Not that he possessed that much either, apart from the Christmas gift basket that was ruining his day. He sometimes thought that life, merely due to the fact that one accepted it, ought to guarantee a friend to play squash with, another to be able to share secrets with over a warming drink or two, and a woman who would love him with the passion of a bacchante. Even though he admitted he might be able to struggle on without the first two, he knew he would need the resolve of a hermit to survive without the third. Taking another sip of the brandy, he closed his eyes and as a joke, since it was the day before Christmas, he made a wish to the ancient forces of Christmas for the companion he thought he had a right to. And, as if reality had no sense of humor or if his own existence were no more than an old musical comedy, at that moment, a woman's hand settled on his like a warm, sweet butterfly.

Pelayo's eyes widened when he felt the jolt of contact, the burning sensation from another person's skin. His face was a picture of bewilderment at finding the woman of his dreams sitting next to him. She was occupying the seat where the gift basket had been, which was now on the floor between her high heels. One glance at her was enough for him to curse himself for being so imprecise in his wish, because the woman that the Christmas elves had brought him far exceeded his expectations. She was undoubtedly a woman, but one of those man-devouring females; an authentic, urban she-wolf starving for company. She was already running her finger around the rim of his glass and asking him huskily if he had plans for the rest of such a frigid evening, followed by an even colder night. Of course Pelayo had plans, plans he could not get out of: he had to take the gift basket to the little old grandmother's house. He rushed to explain all this in a squeaky, lamenting voice as if he were trying to convince himself that it was really the gift basket preventing him from accepting the woman's offer, and not her layers of makeup, revealing clothes, the contrived sensuality of her thick head of hair, or her menacing gestures, the millenarian hunger in her eyes. That it was the commitment he made to the damned gift basket and not the fear that gripped his innards simply at imagining himself—a defenseless weather vane blown about in the hurricane of her lust—shut in a bedroom with this she-wolf that really forced him to refuse her attractive offer. Under other circumstances, he would not have hesitated for a moment to accept it, given that she seemed to him a truly enchanting and extraordinarily beautiful woman. But right now, unfortunately, he had to be getting along, because he still had to find Calle Rosaleda: Maybe she knew it? The woman observed the nervous Pelayo for a moment before informing him, with a scornful twist of the mouth, which street he had to take. Stammering a thank-you, Pelayo recovered the gift basket and left the pub, trying to ensure his steps reflected a calm he was far from feeling.

Outside the bar, he scurried along the street she had mentioned, getting away as quickly as possible from the bonfire of his manliness: after his woeful display, it was no longer any use laying the blame on life. He was the chief architect of his own misfortune, the only one responsible for the fact that his emotional dossier was still a blank sheet. For once Pelayo tried to distance himself from what had happened, to avoid beating himself up by recalling a scene he could not change, and so quickened his pace beneath the tumorlike sky. A saffron glow lit the horizon, heralding the noisy clatter of thunder, and the clouds were rehearsing a fine rain. Pelayo pulled his coat hood as far up as possible as raindrops began to bounce off it like gallstones and tried to protect the gift basket as best he could.

It took him a good hour to realize that spurned women are capable of the most refined cruelty. Mysteriously, every step he took seemed to be leading him away from the suburbs. This called for some thought. Although he was unwilling to admit it, everything appeared to indicate that the she-wolf had deliberately sent him up the wrong street. He stopped and cursed out loud. He could not bear any more. He thought of handing over the blessed gift basket to the first person he met, setting off for home, taking a shower to get rid of the cold in his bones, and, if the television had nothing better to offer, slicing his wrists with the bread knife to see if things went any better for him in the afterlife. But the recurring image of the grandmother slipped into his mind once more to dissuade him, and so Pelayo grit his teeth and walked back the way he had come until he was at the crossroads near the pub. Once there, he peeped cautiously in the window, but there was no longer any sign of the she-wolf. She was probably devouring some other man with fewer scruples. He examined the crossroads carefully and finally chose the opposite direction to the one the woman had indicated, so convinced was he of her evil intentions.

And he was not wrong. He had only gone a few paces when details began to prick his memory. Pelayo had been here before, toting his briefcase and struggling door to door to gain a commission. It was one of those streets on the outskirts that appear endless, alongside a highway clogged with refrigerated trucks, a place where ugly buildings with decaying facades alternated with empty lots matted with undergrowth and small parks embossed with junkies' needles. Most of the streetlamps had been knocked out by stones, so that the only light came from the moon that peeped through the fog from time to time, as well as from the glow of the many bonfires the local inhabitants were clustered around. From a distance, those individuals with faces cast in orange from the flames did not appear dangerous; they seemed instead to have a certain pastoral charm that Pelayo decided not to disturb, despite the fact that his whole being was crying out for a minute of bonfire warmth.

A smile of triumph spread across his face when he found himself outside the building where the old woman lived. It was a down-at-heel apartment block, its facade blackened by the exhaust from a thousand trucks, its windows linked by a web of ropes, as if its inhabitants boarded one another's homes at night. From the ropes hung, swaying in the wind, the vast and varied catalogue of everything that humanity has at its disposal to cover its indignities.

In a rusty barrel next to the entrance to the block, another bonfire was going full blast. A crowd of people, among whom Pelayo could not distinguish the old woman, were holding their hands to the comfort offered by the fire, which a pair of young shepherds was feeding with lengths of wood. The person supplying the blaze in this way was an athletic young man gleefully wielding an axe as he chopped firewood from broken chairs, ruined tables, and any other useless bits of furniture he was given. Pelayo stood for a few minutes observing them, until he felt ridiculous standing there with his hood and his basket.

The woodcutter's blows followed him into the house like an echo of his own heartbeats. Pelayo climbed the stairs without much thought, in the hope of stumbling across something he might recognize that would tell him on which floor his climb should end. The familiar conjunction of a broken hallway light, a fire extinguisher that had been torn from the wall, and a graffiti of a phallus, accompanied by writing that guaranteed him indescribable pleasure if he agreed to pull his pants down then and there, made him halt on the fifth floor.

Using his recollections as a guide, he went down a very long, stinking corridor intermittently lit by flashes of lightning, until he came to a door with an image of the Virgin Mary above the peephole. This had to be the old woman's door—the door that prevented the smell of mint from spreading down the staircase and impregnating the whole neighborhood with a remarkable freshness, turning it into a kind of sterilized purgatory.

Pelayo cleared his throat and pressed the bell lightly. His gesture brought about an eclipse in the peephole: the old woman was becoming more wary with the years. He brought the gift basket up to his face and opened his lips in a toothpaste commercial–worthy smile. After a moment's pause, which seemed to him eternal, he heard someone drawing back an endless number of bolts. Pelayo was astonished to find himself facing not the grandmother's feeble eyes but confronted by the malevolent gaze of the she-wolf, wearing a housecoat that must once have been blue, and smelling of mints, which left him reeling from impossible conjectures. The woman studied his astonishment and then shook her head, as if she could not believe that reality could accommodate such an absurd scene.

"Come on in, Little Red Riding Hood," she invited him, leading the way down the corridor. Pelayo realized he still had his hood up and snatched it down before following the she-wolf disguised as a grandmother down the twisting passage.

The tiny room they came out into seemed even narrower and sadder than he remembered: the furniture piled on top of itself, the lamp giving off a glow-worm's light, the smell of mint making it seem like an enchanted wood. And however much he peered into the gloom, Pelayo could not see the old woman. When she saw him looking for someone, the she-wolf explained: her mother died three months ago. Pelayo took advantage of another lightning flash to scowl at the portraits on the chest of drawers, where the childhood and youth of the she-wolf were on display. The pieces fit together in his mind with astonishing ease. He shrugged, not knowing what to say. He had arrived too late, but anyway it was obvious that a Christmas basket was greatly needed here, and so he deposited it as solemnly as he could on the table. It produced a symphony of grotesque sounds as it crushed all the sweet wrappings strewn over the surface.

The woman thanked him with a smile. A withered kind of smile that was miles distant from the one that lit up her face in the final photograph on the chest of drawers. A smile that seemed to Pelayo extremely melancholy, little more than a grimace that gave a glimpse of a sorrowful, resigned soul, as neglected as his own in the distribution of happiness. He looked more closely at the she-wolf and was surprised to see in the anemic light that she was incredibly vulnerable, not at all dangerous without makeup, her wild mane of hair sacrificed in a schoolgirl's bun and her shapeliness disguised by the threadbare housecoat. Life seemed to have done a good job of crushing her. Pelayo had no difficulty imagining her returning to the nest, head down, devoting herself to looking after her mother like someone who has found the perfect excuse not to have to go on facing an icy, malevolent world set on defrauding her time and again. He noticed she was looking at him equally intently, as if vainly searching for any duplicity. She seemed surprised that she had stumbled across someone without a mask, that Pelayo was nothing more than what she could plainly see: a shell of a man, whose chest you only had to put your ear to in order to hear the sea of his loneliness.

For a long while they stood there in silence, examining each other closely as they were photographed by the lightning flashes, until finally she said, "I'm sorry about the pub. I was just trying to . . ." and did not know what else to say. Not that this mattered. Pelayo knew from experience that there was no word to define what she was looking for, and that the words that were used always got it wrong or perverted it. No term was suitable enough for their clenched stomachs, their longing for tenderness, their deep need to find someone who could untangle their fears and scare off the monsters.

They leaped on each other then, because there had to be a reason for the Gordian knot of their failures to meet, for the studied way in which they had missed each other in the world outside, only to finally come together in the old lady's little room. Pelayo was not surprised that her kisses tasted of mint, that her caresses were like a soothing balm, or that the collision of two desperately needy souls should produce such an overwhelming love that flung them against the small table and sent the Christmas basket crashing to the floor. Its contents were a riot of colors, the bars of *turrón* smashing, the syrup sweetening the drabness of the floor tiles, the *cava* recreating miniature oceans. He did not resist, allowing himself to be devoured by the she-wolf's ancestral passion with his coat half off, hearing through the window the woodcutter's rhythmic chopping, which no longer had any place in the story, because if there was one thing Pelayo could be sure of after this crazy evening, after the novelesque adventure the gift basket had led him on, it was that what he had been taught at school—that life is a fairy tale—was a fairy tale.

Little Furry Animals

Although she began work at nine in the store beneath her apartment, Laura usually got up at seven, when the day was still untouched. Throwing herself out of bed with a supreme effort of will, wrapped entrancingly in a pink negligee that only served to enhance her generous curves, she would head slightly unsteadily for the bathroom, emerging a short while later in a green tracksuit and with her hair in a tight ponytail that made her head look as aerodynamic as a shark. Then she would go downstairs to run around the block a couple of times, jogging in a flexible, elegant way that delighted the handful of early risers starting their day at first light.

From the paper man in his kiosk to the baker, not to mention the gaggle of pensioners perched on the avenue's benches for that very reason. No one could take their eyes off Laura's harmonious movements, the divine oscillation of breasts and buttocks that were a true sight for sore eyes, a sure sign that God cared for those modest, hardworking devils. With the wild lack of self-awareness typically displayed by splendid women who don't get caught up in their own reflections, Laura aroused the neighborhood's male population by showing them that goddesses also perspire.

Afterward, she would return to her apartment and go back into the bathroom, leaving a trail of sweaty clothes across the floor, like a mollusk abandoning its shell. Turning on the shower, she plunged under the jet of water, letting the icy stream cascade down her precious pink body as she leaned against the tiles, short of breath but pleased—not because she had once more prevented the undesirable accumulation of cellulite, but for the feeling that came after a run that made her feel more alive, uplifted, and tuned in to the world. Then she would soap herself slowly but carefully, voluptuously lingering with the sponge on an intimate area that I suspected every man in the vicinity would die to lather for her.

Eventually, she would reemerge wrapped in a towel, her damp hair hanging loose to her shoulders, and stand in front of her closet to choose the clothes destined that day to lie concealed beneath her store assistant's coat. This never took her long. She would lay the chosen garment on her bed and then, with a knowing, mysterious expression on her face, plunge into the realm of disturbing softness that was her underwear drawer in search of a suitable combination, a thong or more baroque garment that she donned unceremoniously, with those routine gestures women employ when no man is looking—as if my telescope didn't count.

I had been observing her for months from the building opposite, immortalizing on my retinas every instant of her life, from her most private moments to those in the public domain—like the eight busy hours she spends behind the counter at Maika's pet store, where my indomitable gaze could also reach, if I bent over far enough. Risking a slipped disc, or inventing ways of setting up various mirrors, I registered her daily routine, the wasting away of an existence that seemed to have been created for something more constructive than endless days spent selling feed for hamsters or goldfish.

Her daily habits were so well established that, after having a glass of milk—semiskimmed and calcium-enriched, according to the zoom on my telescope—Laura always unbolted the front door of the store at precisely one minute to nine. This was the signal for the morning air to tremble with an animal Babel and an acrid smell of cages and creatures in heat, against which the smell wafting from the next-door bakery could do nothing. It stirred my emotions to see the excitement that gripped the animals as she went through the store switching on lights, calling to them and running her manicured fingernails against the bars of the cages in a languid greeting as she made her way to the stand from which hung the white coat that would restrain her shapely form for the rest of the day. This was the moment for me to abandon my position at the window and start my own life, one that even though it had been devoted for a long while to spying on hers, still involved a few more prosaic tasks I was obliged to carry out, such as translating Dickens and feeding my own animals in the poor excuse for a zoo that had been growing dangerously in my apartment since I began dedicating myself to pursuing her.

At this point, I should admit, even if a quick glance round my apartment would seem to contradict the claim, that I have never liked animals. Now, as a result of my inability to woo someone, they filled every corner; were crammed into cages or fish tanks; scampered about or lay listlessly in heaps; wrapped themselves around me; choked me, singly or in flocks; as if they were the stock of a muddle-headed Noah on a dry plateau. Birds, tortoises, dogs, snakes, cats, and other domesticated species lorded over my apartment, lulled by the gurgling of the aquarium giving off the same sharp smell and mosaic of shapes that enveloped Laura, and contemplating in astonishment how each day, after swooshing myself with Brummel cologne and reciting audacious, imaginative declarations of love in front of the mirror, I inevitably returned from the street with a new companion to add to the pile. Of course, this collection of failures demanded almost complete dedication on my part: there was always a cage to be cleaned, an animal to take to the vet, another one to take out to poop in the middle of the sidewalk. As a result, I had long since reduced my tasks for the publishing house to those I could do from home, so that now I earned barely enough for their upkeep by translating the English classics.

Every morning before sitting at my desk, I undertook the laborious ritual of the daily feed: I would fill the trays of *Well, they say it's going to rain this afternoon*, a diamond turtledove that stared at me fascinated from its orange-ringed eyes; of *How nice your hair smells*, a cockatoo that staggered constantly up and down its cage like a drunkard; of *She'll never notice a guy like me*, a Gloster Fancy canary that nodded thoughtfully, its crest flattened like a latter-day Beatles fan; plumped up the straw for *Do you like French cinema?*, a chinchilla that let the days go by rolled up in a dark gray pompom, sleeping so solemnly and determinedly it seemed to be caught up in a labor of cosmic dimensions, possibly that of dreaming the world containing us all; and filled the bowl of *Oh, to hold you in my arms . . .* , a squirrel that, to judge by the impetuous way it looped the loop within the narrow dimensions of its cage, seemed to suggest I was feeding it cocaine. I gave a daily dose of worms to *Today I dreamed of you again*, a statuesque basilisk lizard constantly stuck to the glass of its tank with the slenderest of fingers like struts on an umbrella; and sprinkled plankton on the aquarium, where, performing like a troupe of seasoned folklore dancers, *Tomorrow, tomorrow*, a hyperactive wasp fish, and *Keep the change*, a guppy that draped its tail's embossed mantilla across the aquatic stage, lived. And finally, though only when necessary, I became the implacable demigod of my miniature universe: I would pick up the hamster that had been fattening all week long and lay it as an offering in the terrarium of *I'll take it because I need someone to give me a hug at night. Aha, that's a joke*, a python, that soon began to slither toward it and perform its cruel morning rite—the grim warning that reminded all the other animals that there was a harsher world outside, a ruthless, dangerous one they would do better to remain ignorant of.

My rounds complete, I would collapse into my desk chair, but scarcely had time to get my breath back before I felt the avid licking on the palms of my hands of my seven dogs, clustering around me in the hope of that day being the one I would choose to take for a walk. Exhausted, unable to move, I contemplated the increasingly elaborate wriggling of *It's true, it didn't rain in the end*, a dachshund that squirmed around the floor like a rolling pin, trying to ingratiate himself, the rascal, to get a walk out of me rather than a smile. I glanced at all the other animals looking back at me sympathetically, as if this life outside a cage seemed even more sad and inconsequential than their own.

Their ridiculous nicknames were the encrypted history of our nascent romance, our incomprehensible, tortuous love story. They were both my memory and my frustration. Each of them represented a failed declaration, an attempt at imposing myself that came to nothing, a humorless joke. Inopportune phrases, thoughts formed in the dark silence of my shyness, snatches of conversation that my lack of courage and my ineptness at courtship prevented from securing a date.

I looked again at the dogs, resigned to responding to those ludicrous names that sounded to them like suspicious passwords when I muttered them in the middle of the night. They patiently awaited my verdict. I chose the dachshund. The others accepted my decision in a dignified manner, although one or more of them could not contain a sorrowful moan. Only *Are you really happy?*, the Doberman, stayed aloof in a corner, as though deaf to the complaints of the common crowd, sure in the knowledge that he would be chosen for the evening stroll. His martial, sadistic air would be what his timorous master wanted at the end of the leash. Patrolling the darkness with that hunk of a dog protected me from the taunts of the young skinheads sprawling all over the benches on the avenue, keen to demonstrate how effective their switchblades were.

With the dachshund, of course, things were different. His ridiculous gait meant I only ever took him out by day, when the only others out walking their dogs were the little old ladies with their groomed poodles, from whom the charming waddle of *It's true, in the end it didn't rain* elicited tender, motherly smiles, and occasionally a question as to his sex, sniffing the prospect of obtaining a cross with their own pet, a cuddly circus aberration they could display on their laps and astound any visitors with. I usually deposited the dachshund on the sidewalk just long enough for him to lessen his longing for wide-open spaces, but that morning, feeling a nostalgic twinge, I decided to offer us a few more minutes prowling round Laura's shop. Hiding discreetly behind a lamppost, I watched her hard at work beyond a window full of tortoises and parrots, in the midst of whom there was usually some exotic animal that the passersby gawped at with a mixture of bewilderment and surprise, as if it were some alien creature acting as a scout for some high command winging its way through space toward us. I sometimes thought Maika brought these oddities exclusively for me, just so that every day I would discover a fresh reason to go into her shop and continue my protracted courtship, which always ended up benefiting her when I purchased her latest extravagance, be it a toucan or a tarantula.

At that moment, I always felt a stab of injustice: yet again, it seemed to me Laura had wasted her life, that she could have a glorious or at least more worthy fate, a reasonable destiny that perhaps we could go in search of together. But I soon stumbled across the image reflected in her window of a funny-looking guy with a sausage dog and asked myself what providence could have planned for such a loser as him, what he was expected to do or bring to the world's frenzied activity. And I ended up asking myself for the umpteenth time—fleeing from the particular to the general, which was much less painful—whether we really were guaranteed at birth an interesting and convincing destiny, or if we all came into the world without any concrete mission imprinted on our chromosomes, simply to make up the numbers, to get in each other's way, with the result that it was those few who did manage to do something with their lives for the common good that were the anomalies, the castoffs of a God who loathed any kind of coherence.

Whenever I reflected on people's destiny, I ended up recalling Hurtado, the publishing house's martyr. Hurtado was one of the firm's most brilliant translators, a big, jolly fellow whose head was bald apart from a few tufts, and who had the moustache of a Mexican dictator. Everyone predicted a brilliant future for him, a life that would benefit many others, for which reason his mother, whom I imagined as larger-than-life and fun-loving as him, had torn him from her womb with a proud gesture of maternal pride, mixing groans with curses. This was why we were so taken aback when Hurtado demonstrated so personally and graphically that his destiny was none other than to choke to death during the firm's New Year's Eve dinner. The translator initiated this macabre revelation over the hors d'oeuvres when he cleared his throat several times in a way that led his neighbor at table to give him a few half-hearted taps on the back, almost absentmindedly. But Hurtado, not content with this meager show of politeness, continued with a crescendo of increasingly noisy, desperate coughs, accompanying them by flinging his arms about and knocking over a couple of glasses. This caught the attention of the other dinner guests, who broke off their conversations and glanced at him curiously, as if trying to work out what kind of party trick the translator was performing, and if it was really worth sacrificing the glassware for. A few made to stand up when Hurtado began to go red in the face and to throw what looked like an astonishingly real fit, but the laughter that others egged him on with left them in two minds. All of a sudden, after a tremendous whistling sound, the translator collapsed across the table, facedown in the punch bowl, like an animal arriving at a water trough. A sepulchral silence crystallized in the room. We all turned our eyes toward Don Vigueira, the publisher. Urged on by our stares, he rose from the head of the table and approached his collapsed minion with great caution, as if afraid that Hurtado was planning suddenly to spring upright and top off his silly joke by putting the wind up his boss. It was only when Don Vigueira's fingers found no pulse on Hurtado's carotid that he seemed to relax. Hurtado had fallen off his perch, just like that, in mid-dinner, despite all the many appointments in his diary. Later we were told that all that effort had burst a blood vessel, flooding his lungs with blood. The translator's sudden death meant that the dinner was suspended, and most of the guests left somewhat shaken to welcome in the New Year somewhere less doom-laden. Only the executives and a few curious bystanders with nothing better to do stayed on to await the ambulance. As it made its way through the traffic, I was observing Hurtado, who had been laid out on the sofa with a handkerchief covering his face, either to preserve him from our rude scrutiny or to protect us from the ghastly grimace that distorted his features. This absurd end to his days led me to wonder about our role in the universe's complex intrigues. How could it permit a man to construct his life, to plan his existence so carefully and hopefully, without warning him of such an unexpected, grotesque end? Was that why Hurtado had come into this world—to choke to death at a party, giving the other guests such a spectacular demonstration of the precariousness of existence? There, face-to-face with the translator's corpse,

I began to imagine a more just world, where the newborn, after receiving the doctor's slap, would be handed over to a fortune-teller to accurately predict their future so that those whom the whims of fickle fate did not allow to attain a fulfilled existence could decide how best to administer the fleeting time they had on this Earth. It was obvious that if the fortunate ones that ended their fertile days dying in bed were carried off by a majestic, hooded reaper with a scythe, Hurtado had been summoned by death dressed as a buffoon, a hunchback with bells on his cap. After that, the idea that everyone came into the world with a joyful destiny under his arm seemed to me a romantic illusion.

Seen from this point of view, anything might happen to Laura and me, but I trusted that in spite of everything our destinies, whatever they might be, would merge at some point along the way. I was so convinced of this that, even though the wait was seriously undermining my current account and I could sense that sooner or later there was bound to be an animal I was allergic to, I cheerfully accepted it, telling myself whenever I became impatient that it was the years of aging that guaranteed the quality of the wine. Therefore, our slow-motion falling in love comforted rather than frustrated me. Neither Laura nor I needed any third person to come along and speed things up.

Segismundo could just as well have stayed home. But he had to appear, with his mop of hair and his beard, his thread-bare jeans and his T-shirts with their ecological slogans, to parade through the neighborhood with his commitment to grunge and hand out his awareness-raising leaflets to all and sundry. Until finally, when perhaps he caught sight of the beauty that looked after the repugnant pet store, he burst into the shop as if in a trance, disembarking in Laura's life knowing he was expected, like some biodegradable Prince Charming determined to make her hair stand on end with his dramatic tales of animals on the verge of extinction.

I never found out where he built his lair, but I began to see him increasingly often in the pet shop, leaning on the counter like a barfly, telling the customers—but especially Laura—about his environmental battles. Not even if I had overcome my shyness or trained my tongue in the art of oratory would I have been able to rival the seductive images Segismundo conjured up before the eyes of the assistant and anyone else that cared to listen. He looked so scrawny and insignificant, but then went on to describe the time when he was part of the crew of the *Rainbow Warrior*, the Greenpeace boat that used to sail between the whaling ships and their prey; how he had spent days clinging to the anchors of countless boats carrying nuclear waste, slowing down with his stubbornness the world leaders' underhanded games. Of course, it went without saying that he had also been in Kenya protecting elephants from ivory poachers; had fought in the Amazon on the side of the trees; had seen, like someone watching television, how a lioness gave birth to her cub on the grasslands of the savannah; and had freed a grizzly from a trap, so that now he had a blood brother three meters tall and four hundred kilos in weight that fished salmon with a swipe of his paw in some corner of Alaska; and with his heart in his mouth he had witnessed the amazing sight of hundreds of young penguins leaping off the edge of an iceberg into the icy waters in search of a mouthful of food or death from starvation. In other words, he had seen everything the animal world had to offer and everything the world of man did not. As described in Segismundo's alcohol-sodden voice, the planet was a bigger place, a vast expanse, a constant surprise package where marvels and tragedies coexisted in an inharmonious harmony, the joke of a God that a handful of crusaders like him were at pains to defend.

Hidden among the sacks of animal feed, I watched him approach the spellbound Laura, drawing as close as possible in a move that almost forced him to sprawl across the counter and talk to her about dream animals that would never fill her cages, and which at that very moment—and at this point he would click his fingers dramatically—were ceasing to exist because of a bullet fired from the undergrowth, a sacrilegious projectile that had slowly ripened in the shotgun of the greatest predator on Earth. One species of animal disappears every quarter of an hour, he affirmed indignantly. And, as though declaring his love for her, Segismundo told her of the Siberian tiger hunted for its skin, of the turtle served as a delicacy in luxury restaurants, of the Tasmanian tiger, not seen since the 1980s. He wooed her with whales, whose brain grease she probably smeared on her face; the armadillo, under threat because its habitat was being devastated; the spiny anteater, used as a shooting target in some areas of Paraguay; the marsh deer, whose antlers were displayed as trophies; and almost all the primates, sold to laboratories for biomedical experiments. A requiem that every morning included different species, but which Segismundo always rounded off with the same terrifying pronouncement: over the past three hundred years, man had multiplied a thousandfold the rate of extinction of natural processes.

And these improvised ecological lectures began to have their effect, to inject the poison of remorse for doing nothing into Laura's previously carefree existence. Through my telescope, I soon noticed that this girl belonged to that minority of people who carry within them an impressionable, committed soul in which the problems of the world—and in particular those of the environment—strike home with astonishing ease. It took only a mention of them to make her turn against herself, to make her sizzle on her bed like drops of water in boiling oil. From that moment on, Laura flung herself up in the morning with a tortured soul and ran to complete her ablutions as quickly as possible in order to sweep from her mind the remaining cobwebs of a night's sleep that instead of bringing calm had been a torment. Thanks to the prophecies about the devastating effects of climate change on the majority of the planet's natural habitats—which the newscaster had seemed almost embarrassed to murmur after passionately listing the new transfers for the soccer season—her peaceful dreams had

transformed into ghastly nightmares: an anguished procession
of polar bears, seals, and caribou expiring in a resigned and
harrowing silence in their realms of melting ice. But not even
her morning run could soothe her. Those troubled awakenings
and her frequent absentmindedness behind the counter only
served to underline the power Segismundo had over her. It
was no use to pawn my hours of sleep to learn more about
the animal kingdom from the four or five encyclopedias I
had checked out of the library, because I could only reel off
the information in front of her as urgently as someone pro-
nouncing a lifesaving spell, without ever endowing my words
with the charm and naturalness of someone who had lived
the experience. It was plain that all was lost. After months
and months of observing the boring sway of my hook, Laura
had decided to swallow the fresh bait destiny was dangling
in front of her. It was only a matter of time, and much less
time than I imagined, before she discovered she was in love
with that dubious ecologist. The morning I confirmed that
painful truth I bought from her a Pekingese that found it hard
to respond to the name of *Maybe the man of your life has
always been right in front of you*.

Finally, a couple of nights later, the fateful moment arrived.
Circles always close, for good or ill. I was spying on her Saturday afternoon with a bitter grimace on my face when, at
about eight o'clock, Laura, who had spent hours slumped on
the sofa, seemed to come back to life and became frenetically
active. She was busy with her oven, showered and perfumed

herself carefully, put on some music, and as a finishing touch lit the candles she had placed on the table. I didn't need any further clues: her courtship had lasted exactly a month, like that of penguins, a period of elaborate nuptial singing that was now reaching its climax. With tears in my eyes, I watched her pace nervously round her apartment, dressed up like a princess for another man, awaiting the arrival of her champion, who suffered on behalf of every shot eagle, every chopped-down fir tree. I felt sorry for her. Laura had not yet been taught enough harsh lessons by life and, like the tadpoles of the *Oophaga pumilio* frog, had not yet had time to secrete her poisonous toxins, making her an easy prey for any predator.

Shortly afterward, lowering the telescope, I saw him arrive, strolling along wearily with his washed-out jeans and his unkempt hair, like someone coming to collect payment for all the saliva he had spent. Just like the Bengal tiger, Segismundo hunted at night. He advanced furtively, upwind, and did not bring any wine to the table. My only wish was that Laura did not give herself to him as soon as she opened the door, that she might make him sweat a little before surrendering in a swoon, because there was a possibility that the ecologist would have no patience and that like a puma he favored lightning attacks, a powerful leap that lasted only a few seconds before exhausting itself. But Segismundo was a cunning old fox. He looked on poker-faced when Laura, no longer in her shop coat but perched atop high heels and squeezed into a dress with more-than-generous cleavage, ushered him into her lair.

Even so, I could see he was excited at being presented with a shapelier body than he had been expecting, although he took the glass she offered him with a polite smile. He knew he had won before the game even started. Now he had to rein in his instincts, to control himself even if it was painful, to avoid at all costs flinging her onto the table and taking what was already his in the midst of ferocious growls. He had to pick the fruit without hurrying, allowing it to fall from the tree by its own weight. And so he was unfailingly well behaved throughout the dinner, only permitting himself to look her up and down with lustful eyes when she asked if he'd like a dessert. Laura lowered her head, blushing and submissive, like female crocodiles do when they smell the male's musk.

Segismundo was an independent, solitary sort, who, like, a panda, only gave up his solitude during the mating season. Then he sought out the closest female and competed with the nearby males for her. He had seen me off a long time since, and so Segismundo wiped the crumbs from his beard and finally stood up to claim his prize. The moment had come to spill something more than saliva. They went at it like wolves, launching themselves into a struggle that was all biting and gentle licking, until Segismundo seemed to grow bored with all this carrion-eating preamble and took up his position to the rear, where he sealed his efforts at seduction via the narrow channel, with sudden, doglike thrusts that lasted close to thirty minutes.

Disgusted, I dropped the telescope. What now? When we love a woman we cannot have, there are only two alternatives:

to forget or to become obsessed. And I had the whole night in front of me to choose between the two options. The animals gave me worried looks. In return, I offered them a strained smile, so that they would see I was fine, that I could take it, that life had long since immunized me against emotional traumas. That I had them. I don't know how convincing I was. Contemplating my pets while the woman I loved was sleeping with a man who wasn't me, I came to the philosophical conclusion that emotions were like animals: they came in all shapes and sizes and conditions, and you had to take care of them, feed them every day, clean them regularly. They lived in freedom among the trees, like native spirits, until someone captured them and shut them in a cage of devotion and timidity. And doubtless many of them did not survive. I could rid myself of the pain in my chest that my love for Laura had become in recent days—like someone abandoning a dog in a ditch—or I could go on feeding that angry animal until the cage it was in grew so old it fell to pieces. It was my decision.

The next morning, Laura got out of bed at seven, careful not to disturb the sleep of her lover, who was snoring away like a sated beast. She put on her tracksuit, went out into the street, and began her morning run. By the pale light of dawn, Laura ran like never before, possessed by a schoolgirl enthusiasm that made me want to vomit. My car was waiting for her at the end of the street, engine running, like a wild animal ready to pounce. I wouldn't either forget her or become obsessed by her. The dark paths of the night had led me to a third conclusion. Not without a certain sorrow, I had come to see that after all our destiny was not to love one another, or to choke to death during an end of year party. Maybe I had been put on this Earth to kill the woman I loved, and maybe she had been predestined to a mysterious, untimely death—that of being knocked down by a hit-and-run driver. Unfortunately, that's how things stood: I could see Laura now in my rearview mirror, as if she were coming for an appointment, smiling in a way that was the opposite of the pain I felt. My heart was beating wildly and my hands stuck to the steering wheel with that cold sweat we only get when we have hepatitis or at crucial moments in our lives.

I remember that day as one of exhausting sadness and acceptance. Laura, my beloved Laura, is no longer with us. She has gone to a better place. Whenever I pass by the pet store with my new dog, a spotty twentysomething stares back at me suspiciously from behind the counter. All circles close, more or less satisfactorily. I get on with my life: I translate Dickens and take walks round the neighborhood, and at night I delve into the garbage of the news to see if I can spot her face somewhere in the world, fighting to save seals or whales, or any other lost cause. And curled up at my feet, dozing all the time, is the Dalmatian, the last animal I bought from her before Segismundo appeared with suitcases to fulfill her destiny. A Dalmatian that is already starting to answer to its name: *I couldn't do it.*

The Brave Anesthetist

One summer's morning, a tailor was sitting at his table by the window, merrily sewing away, for he was in an exceedingly good mood, when a peasant woman came down the street peddling her wares:

"Lovely preserves for sale! Lovely preserves for sale!"

To the tailor's ears, this sounded like heavenly music. He poked his head through the window and called out to her. Laden with her heavy baskets, the woman mounted the stairs to the tailor's house, where he demanded to see all her jars. The tailor examined them carefully, thrusting his nose into each one. Perhaps he was tempted to dip his finger in them too—his forefinger, if not his thumb—to extract the sweet jam and daub it on the woman's lips, accompanying this impertinence with the smile of an aging Lothario. For, regardless of whether he stitched for a living, the tailor was still a man, and no man can escape his condition, Elenita dear.

It's best you learn this now, my love. That way you will suffer less. There is little or no difference between a man and a rat. At first, you may find this hard to believe, because men are clever and know how to disguise it. But as soon as you turn into the beautiful young woman your looks predict, armies of them will assail you, concealing their verminous natures behind cheap smiles and expensive gifts. Once they have what they want, you will see how the best of them succumb to inertia, while the worst don't even bother to go through the motions. They simply tear away their mask, revealing themselves to you unequivocally as selfish, insensitive, and above all disloyal.

And so, Elena my dear, if this were real life instead of a children's story, the tailor would be unable to resist the temptation to find out whether he was still attractive or not; whether all those gray hairs hadn't simply lent him a dignified air; and that in his wife's fortnightly caresses there wasn't after all a hint of repulsion, or obligation, as he had started to suspect of late. He would smear his forefinger, if not his thumb, in apricot, and thus smothered would raise it to the lips of the preserve seller. She in turn would receive it calmly, with good humor, engaging her tongue, abandoning herself as though in a trance to her energetic licking. For if this were real life and not a children's story, Elenita dear, there is no doubt that the preserve seller would be a young woman in her twenties, the type who knows the value of a pair of swaying hips and a plunging neckline. The sort of floozy that preys on older, married men who shower them with wisdom and promises. And by the time they cross the threshold, feel the warm embrace of luxury, see money winking at them wherever they look, they will already have employed all their wiles to banish any remorse the man might feel, transforming him in the blink of an eye into a slave of his desire. For if this were real life, the only strange thing about the story would be that the slut wasn't selling encyclopedias instead of those stupid preserves.

The story might seem less appealing, more insipid, without the forefinger, if not his thumb, rummaging inside the young woman's fresh mouth, like a snail leaving a slimy trail of apricot. But the two of them would find a way to turn the act of browsing through an encyclopedia into a crescendo of caresses that could only end in a writhing possession on the dining room table, on the polished plank of mahogany where his wife and daughter sat down to eat every day, and at Christmas, his in-laws. That was where he was discovered, engaged in the treacherous penetration, deep in lace underwear, trousers round his ankles, his scrawny, hairy behind, never before illuminated from that angle, by that light accustomed only to embracing anodyne Sunday scenes.

Not that the tailor was careless, or indeed even a tailor, incapable as he was of sewing on a button, but an anesthetist, Elenita dear, just like your father. A man whose job is simply to prepare the way for the surgeon, despite his attempts to give his profession a philosophical meaning; the bastard Morpheus, as I used to call him, although nowadays I'd just call him a bastard. No, he wasn't a careless person; on the contrary, he couldn't have been more methodical, to the point where the alarm clock hardly dared go off since he was already on his feet. He even went bald in an orderly fashion, his hairs falling out one by one. That's why I am sure he abandoned himself to that coupling in the way he did, not bothering to look at his watch with that repulsive self-assurance of his, simply glancing at the position of the sun, three-quarters of an hour away from gilding the arm of the sofa. He abandoned himself with the nonchalance of a schoolboy, knowing exactly how much time he had, scrupulously dispensing the coming minutes—so many for the frantic copulation, so many for the postcoital embrace, a generous amount for her to put on her clothes without the kind of urgency that might emphasize the clandestine nature of the situation. And a few more seconds, just to be on the safe side, in case the girl proved excessively clingy and he had to reach for his checkbook. I'd like to believe that's what it was like, Elenita dear, that testing out his prowess on a young body was enough for him, and that he wouldn't try to prolong their brief encounter, much less fall under the spell of all that crude adolescence, that he would never dream of throwing away fifteen years of marriage.

Of course this is the same story Daddy was reading to you, my sweet! Come along, close your eyes and try to fall asleep. Mummy has had a bad day, and she wants to go to bed too. Where was I? Oh yes, now comes the part about the flies.

In the story, the tailor said goodbye to the girl, and used her preserves for strictly culinary purposes—that's to say, he spread them chastely on a slice of bread. But his plan was spoiled by flies, naturally, a sort of plague sent by us women in response to his hypocritical behavior. Because he lied to all those children, made them think he was impervious to his inescapable, base instincts, he is now forced to contemplate the revolting troupe marching across his breakfast, some of them already camped out on the layer of apricot. In the end, the tailor seized a piece of cloth and used it to swipe at the affronted slice. When he pulled it back, he could see several insects encrusted in the preserves like amber decorations, affirming their miniscule existences with a tiny flutter of wings. He counted seven of them. And he considered this an extraordinary feat, worthy of being shared with the entire city.

Thus, without further ado, he set about embroidering on a crimson sash the words *Seven with one blow*, then took to the streets so that everyone could read of his achievement. Which is doubtless what your father would have done, Elenita dear, if only he hadn't been found out. For that is what men are: creatures that need to show off their accomplishments; vain troubadours crooning about their exploits, in particular their sexual conquests. They even have places specially designed for these confessions, from squalid nightspots to sophisticated clubs, where they exchange lavish details of their adventures between desultory games of poker. And how many membership cards to such places did your father carry around in his wallet? How many scenes from his early morning joust might he have chosen to recount to his sweaty palms had the meticulous anesthetist not been foolish enough to marry a woman given to sudden bouts of forgetfulness, to cultivating a whole host of oversights, whose unpredictability he might have tried to map using color charts or computer programs so that in one of his diaries he could assign a day and an hour to my future lapses of memory?

Clearly, he had predicted none that morning, judging from the look of surprise on his face when he saw me standing there, silent, bewildered; I would even say submerged in spiritual contemplation, framed opportunely by the doorway like a virgin in a niche. And you'd be surprised, Elena dear, how many things can go through a wife's mind when she contemplates the spectacle of her husband beavering away between another woman's legs. My devastating shock gave way to the most overwhelming horror; I veered from icy hatred to burning rage, instantly followed by searing shame, then clinical analysis, and ending with a surprising anamorphosis. Because, viewed from that unusual angle, the nodding donkey of that backside looked to me exactly like a huge, fleshless skull.

I didn't know what to do. I didn't know what to say. No word or gesture seemed appropriate to the scene, but I couldn't simply fetch Don Zambrano's documents and leave. Then my eye alighted on the green marble ashtray on the side table, and all at once I understood why we had never thrown it away, irrespective of how ugly it was and that neither of us smoked anymore. I realized then that the secret destination of that ashtray was your father's skull, that it had been waiting with deadly patience to smash his head in, managing to pass unnoticed despite its size and garish color. As I raised it and took aim, I remembered with fondness the strange little man who had come to our wedding bearing that gift, had stood in a corner nibbling on some crayfish, and then disappeared, leaving the rest of us with only the mystery of his shy presence and the shells from his modest feast. And yet, despite the galvanizing force of my hatred, the ashtray traced an unfortunate arc far above your father's head and crashed into the aquarium. After the impact, the sea appeared to spew onto the carpet.

The noise distracted the lovers, who both puzzled over the source of the wriggling fish writhing about the floor. It was the anesthetist who spotted me first from his prone position, and, arms flailing as if he were wading through thick mud, he hurriedly dismounted the girl in pursuit of respectable verticality. After the laborious decoupling, he stood before me, a confused hominid, ridiculously tragic in the midst of the gasping fish. He looked at me warily at first, but then exploded in a wild torrent of words. "This isn't what it seems," he explained, waving his arms about exaggeratedly, as if he had just made the discovery that everything in the world was a mistake, and he wanted to share it. The ashtray wasn't really an ashtray, then? Maybe I had tried to smash his head in with a theater season ticket, or a crab cake? "I can explain," he kept saying, even as the explanation covered up her curvaceous arguments and hurriedly disappeared, having fulfilled her woodworm role. I watched her flee with the prancing grace of a filly, and I longed to be her age, her shape, to accompany her as she continued wreaking havoc on other families, to flee that situation myself, for which I could see no solution. I longed not to be the one destroyed. But that was not possible. We each have our allotted role in life's great tragicomedy, and mine was clearly to stay there, with your father flapping around me, engaged in a tedious monologue of torment that was undermined by his skinny nudity.

My head was throbbing. Suddenly, I felt this was all wrong, absurd. And yet, what else could I expect from such a crazy world, where women with stammers don't have Siamese twins, and no one knows what question flamingos are posing with their necks? I raised my fingers to my temples, but the distressed anesthetist didn't get the message. He pressed on with his heated discourse, because the thing needed to be resolved there and then, in the heat of the moment, before it all coagulated in my head. He talked and talked, sometimes in a pleading tone, at others in the voice of a man of the world, as if he couldn't decide whether to grovel or act casually. It was only when I placed at his feet a suitcase into which I had flung a few of his things that he broke off his speech and announced with a solemn expression that this meant nothing to him, that he still loved me.

So you see, Elenita dear, on top of everything else, I was meant to feel grateful that he had scarcely been implicated in that dog show he had played a starring role in on the table, his unstinting loyalty to me while he was plugging another woman's pussy. The fearless son of a whore.

That's why the fish are no longer in the living room, and why I was late picking you up from school for the first time in eight years. And if there's one thing I'll never forgive your father for, it's your unnecessary tears soaking my handkerchief with the softness of dew. I won't forgive him your sobs, or the look of shock on your teacher's face when she sniffed on my breath the two martinis I had needed to steady my hands on the wheel, the barroom smell that so inexplicably explained my delay. That's why, Elena dear, that's why I've been so subdued all day, secretly drinking in the kitchen; staring at myself in the mirror trying to convince myself that wrinkles are characterful; trying to understand your father, while in the middle of your homework you tried to understand me. And that's why I'm reading you this story, the way your father used to do every night, although God knows I have little desire to do so, for you to go to sleep believing that the world is just as it was before, even if my footsteps padding around the apartment seemed to contradict this.

And where is your father now? He has probably gone to a hotel and is devouring the salted almonds in the minibar, waiting for my anger to subside. Or maybe he is roaming the darkest, loneliest streets, dragging his suitcase and his sins behind him like a ghost consumed with guilt. I can only hope that at some point during his wanderings he bumps into a big ugly brute, which is what has just happened to the tailor in our story. Not a gentle giant who challenges him to throw stones into the sky, and whom he fools by releasing a bird from his pocket, but one encased in bike leathers, dark deeds, and childhood traumas: a professional who realizes that your father's wallet is ripe for the picking the moment he ventures into his territory. And if possible, who wouldn't be content for him to hand over the wallet meekly, but is offended that this makes him feel like a beggar. A giant who can't resist the desire to beat up the anesthetist in a quiet alleyway, disgusted, for example, by his suit—the impeccable cut of which suggests a comfortable, smug life—one of those unashamed lives with a sense of entitlement. And now to the alleyway, to observe the pain and suffering while we still have time. So that the same fate that took him from me in the morning returned him to me in the evening, admittedly all beaten up and remorse-stricken, with the penance of multiple fractures that will take time to heal, and an inner dread that for years will wake him drenched in sweat. The indelible memory of a steel toecap in the ribs.

That's what I want, Elena dear, for your father to suffer the way I have. For the emergency department to call and say, "Señora Cardenas? Look, don't be alarmed, but your husband has suffered—" and for them to break off in mid-sentence. I would calmly put on my lipstick while a cab waits outside, and head to the hospital to find him in pieces on a gurney, crying my name like a drunken sailor, bandaged from head to toe. Except for his hands. Yes, except for his hands, my love, as if the giant had also been bewitched by your father's hands.

I can still remember the first time I saw them, emerging from the jacket sleeves of that ordinary-looking man who approached me in a bar, and who I left with shortly afterward. I remember him offering to buy me a couple of drinks, and accepting reluctantly, tired as I was of being pestered by men, until I looked at his hands. After that, I didn't mind his toad-like eyes, his rabbit teeth, and his unfunny jokes. I wanted to spend the rest of my life contemplating those hands. I wanted to touch them. I wanted them to touch me. They were unbelievably slender, as if they might snap if they held more than one cigarette at a time, and so pale they seemed to give off a moonlit phosphorescence. For a while I was mesmerized, watching them dart across the bar, between the glass and the ashtray, like deep-sea fish. I soon asked him what he did for a living, convinced that with such hands he must surely devote himself to pleasuring angels. As if I had pressed a button, his eyes clouded and his voice grew somber.

"I kill people," he confessed, slowly exhaling his cigarette, "then I bring them back to life. I'm a faux assassin, a pretend criminal, an impotent toreador. I am the eternal siesta, the artificer of death, the commuter train to Hades. I'm not concerned with the material world. I manipulate souls."

That's what he said, just like that, melancholy and remote. Although I was tipsy, I managed to arch my eyebrows gracefully, and he knew that he had me. He went on to explain, moving his ivory hands like a conjurer without cards, that while the surgeon was mired in the mud of flesh, he captured the essence of the spirit, hooked it on his line, and with a nimble flick of his wrist cast it into the abyss, only to rescue it enveloped in supernatural vapors, soaked in God's own breath. I didn't mind being one of many women bewitched by his brooding reflections. All I wanted was to feel those porcelain hands on my body, hands that that very morning had doubtless hovered over some patient, gently lulling them to sleep with an infusion of ether, while binding them to the world with threads of oxygen. That night we ended up in his apartment anaesthetized by love, enveloped in a pleasure-induced narcosis. And the sight of his hands running over my body like albino mice was so beautiful that I decided there and then that no one else would ever caress me, that those shimmering hands could explore my mud forever, even if that was only possible with the aid of Pentothal.

And so, my sweet, after several chapters in which the tailor reveals how quick-witted he is, he finally succeeds in marrying the princess and inheriting a kingdom. And everyone lives happily ever after, because that's the reason for fairy tales.

But what if there was no call from the hospital, Elena dear? What if when the telephone rang, I picked up the receiver and heard your father's voice curled up in a ball, repeating my name like a moist prayer, savoring each syllable, clawing at the letters like a man in love? What would I do, Elenita darling? Would I keep this up, or would I forgive him, so that our lives could carry on resembling a children's story?

So why doesn't he call?

Meows

For Juan Bonilla, who endured the first part of this story.

I can't see it from the terrace, so I don't know how big it is, or what color. The only thing I know is that every night, perched up on the roof, it wails my name at the moon. I'm no cat expert, but I think it must be in heat. It sounds like a heartbroken child. I could even describe it as terrifying. It reminds me of the screams of those pale creatures locked in basements in horror films. And I'm increasingly convinced it's mewling my name.

Of course, I'd love a second opinion. Someone I could ask: *Hey, listen, don't you think that cat is mewling my name?* But Virginia left me two months ago, before it began, as stealthily as she had come into my life. On a day like any other, she set off to buy lettuce to restock my bare fridge and never returned, even though that very same morning, her body entwined with mine, she had assured me that now that she had found me, she would never leave.

After her flight, I regretted that the two months of passion we had spent shut up in my apartment, far from the outside world, had left me with nothing more useful than happiness: no phone number, address, or surname to complement the first name that, once she had disappeared, I found myself compulsively muttering at all hours of the day like a spell that no longer conjured her up. But that was how she had wanted it: two naked souls, stripped of their everyday identities and impurities, each yearning for the other. She wanted her body, her green-flecked eyes, her damp hair, to be enough for me; for me to know nothing whatsoever about her when we weren't together. She wanted a love apart from the world, outside even of time, free from the bonds of circumstance—a love composed solely of flesh and blood and electric skin. There would be plenty of opportunities later for all the rest, all the stuff that would make us worldly and wise and other. The stuff that would probably destroy us. And I accepted her conditions, which revealed her to me as she wished to be seen: a wood sprite, an elfin being, the last throwback to a mythical lineage garlanded with fairies, fauns, and elves, and about whom the only thing I needed to know was that she loved me like no one else ever had or ever would. Although, had I suspected that one fine day she would simply vanish into thin air, I would have asked for every last detail, down to her dentist's address. That way I could have sought her in more accessible and obvious places than in an enchanted wood.

Virginia, the woman who vowed she would never leave me, disappeared one afternoon about two months ago. Ever since, I've been unable to sleep at night. Darkness descends on the city, and from my bed I watch the world, which in those small hours emits only the creaking sounds of a drifting ship: the snorting fridge, the metallic belch of the elevator secretly running through the bowels of the building, a solitary car horn in the distance like the lament of a dying man. I listen to it all conscientiously, but above all I listen for the cat, the only living being apart from me that seems to be awake in this corner of the universe.

Had I been called Evaristo, Froilan, or Salustiano, perhaps things would have been easier. Cats find names like that impossible to pronounce. But my name is Juan, like my father, like my grandfather, like the fictitious Don Juan Tenorio. And the cat seems to be aware of this, for every night, with startling punctuality, she turns up on the roof and desperately, painfully, calls to me. Like someone calling her lover.

I don't want to believe that I'm right, because it could well be the first step toward losing my mind. But the truth is, I can't help it. I spend the whole day obsessed, waiting for nightfall, when I will get another chance to prove that I'm mistaken, that I'm not mad, and that the cat is not really calling my name. Yet each time I hear more clearly that she is mewling my name: *Juan, Juan* . . . Tirelessly, yearningly.

I'm the only Juan in the apartment building. I've checked the mailboxes. There are dozens of Antonios, numerous Pedros and Luises, even a Froilan, but no Juan. If that cat is calling to anyone, it has to be me. I'm the one she's looking for. There's no other possibility.

The fourth time I heard her, fearful that she was turning me into an insomniac, I decided to act. I knocked on some of the doors. Apparently, no one hears a cat mewling desperately in the middle of the night, but this might be because I am the only occupant on the top floor. In the end, someone gave me a clue: maybe she belonged to our new neighbor, the girl who had just moved into the building.

Ever since Virginia left me, I've turned my back on the world, so I was not surprised to discover we had a new neighbor of whom I knew nothing. In my current state of self-absorption, I'd only have noticed her arrival if they had dragged a grand piano up the stairs for her. But the new neighbor arrived without musical accompaniment, muffled in the insulation of a dense silence. And from the balcony I assumed was hers, no cat would have had trouble reaching the roof. I could have done it myself. I think there can be no doubt about who the little pussycat that ruins my nights belongs to.

I resolve to put an end to my ordeal and ring her doorbell the following afternoon. I can't decide whether the woman who answers is beautiful or not, but she seems attractive enough. Thin, not too tall, one of those women who would go to her grave with a smile. Based on her clothes—a tight-fitting crop top that exposes her pierced navel—and the sweat beading under her arms, I deduce that I've interrupted a workout. Perhaps she was running on a treadmill or doing sit-ups on one of those contraptions you can store folded up beneath the bed, where in olden times a chamber pot used to be kept. I've always admired the kind of woman who can set aside a few hours a day to sculpt her body, possibly because I count myself among those who leave their shape to chance and the wind. But I know nothing could possibly ever happen between us, because we're condemned to start off on the wrong foot.

I politely inquire whether she has a cat. A female cat, she confirms. Even more politely, I suggest she stick a ballpoint pen up the cat's rectum, because I'm utterly fed up with hearing her mewling every night. But, as is well-known, we don't live in a world where we can freely express ourselves. The woman's smile vanishes, and she stares at me as if I had just dropped squid guts onto her fresh laundry. The dark circles under my eyes don't seem to affect her. With infinite politeness, she informs me that, despite the fact that she would be more than happy to introduce a ballpoint pen—or any similar sharp object—into my rectum, she has not the least intention of doing so to her cat's. Earplugs are available from any pharmacy, she concludes, and starts to shut the door.

That is when the pussycat appears. And that changes everything. What can I say? The sight of her moves me greatly. She's a white cat, of such a delicious whiteness that I can't help thinking that some extremely skilled craftsman made her out of a snowball. She is neither plump nor emaciated, with a light, lissome body. And her eyes are of an indefinable green verging on yellow. But what surprises me most is the way she behaves. The cat stands stock-still in the kitchen doorway and studies me with a mixture of mistrust and rapture. Finally, she overcomes her paralysis and advances slowly toward me with measured steps, as if I were some apparition that might vanish at any moment. When she reaches me, she rubs against my legs with such sincere affection it makes me uncomfortable. Her rhythmic and ecstatic rubbing provokes a vague quiver of excitement. I pick her up and look into her eyes.

"Why do you call out to me? What do you know about me?" I ask in a whisper, so the woman won't hear me.

The cat says nothing. She restricts herself to staring at me with a look that appears to conceal another behind it, a double look. My neighbor breaks the silence. "I don't believe it," she says, shaking her head as if she has seen a miracle. "It's the first time she's behaved like this with someone she doesn't know. She's usually hostile. She doesn't let anyone come near her, let alone pick her up."

I return the cat to the floor, from where she goes on staring at me, as if she wants to be sure I got the message. But what message? What is she trying to tell me?

"Would you like a coffee?" asks the woman, friendly all of a sudden.

I accept and she asks me in, still expressing her amazement, in a rushed outpouring, at the pussycat's extraordinary behavior. It's obvious she's only just moved in, because the passage to the living room is a real obstacle course: crates, bags, and filing cabinets block the hallway and spill into corners. She invites me to sit down on a narrow sofa in front of a table improvised from a closet door and a few bricks.

"I'm going to put on the coffee and take a shower. Make yourself comfortable."

I try to obey, but it's hard to make yourself comfortable with a cat in front of you that won't stop scrutinizing you with a disconcertingly fixed stare. She has a gaze that could trip up a trapeze artist; render sleepwalkers self-conscious; make a man ask himself why no woman has ever looked at him like that. I feel obligated to respond to her attention, but how? Meanwhile, her owner is busying herself in the kitchen preparing the coffee. From the amount of noise she makes, it would have been less work to build a pyramid. In the end, just as I am considering venturing into the kitchen to inquire whether she might need assistance in undertaking such a complicated procedure, I hear the water start to run in the shower. Her cat and I continue to study each other, without knowing what to say. I wonder whether the animal is absorbed in the same thoughts as me, or if I am attributing to her a sensitivity and intelligence she doesn't possess. After all, she's only a cat. But why doesn't she seem like that to me? Why do I have the unnerving feeling that for her being a cat is only an assumed role, a disguise?

I'm absorbed in these reflections when the girl reappears, wrapped in a yellow bathrobe and carrying a little tray with two cups on it. As she walks over to the sofa, the garment intermittently falls open, like the curtain of a puppet show, to reveal a pair of soft pink thighs. I'd hardly be human if my pulse didn't quicken when I notice that the only thing protecting the rest of her body is the precarious knot she has fastened the bathrobe with, a knot that could so easily slip even in the hands of an idiot like me, useless at origami or cardiovascular surgery. Casually, she begins to serve the coffee, as though unaware of the sensuality exuded by her damp hair and the scent of soap on her skin, but I wasn't born yesterday: I know she is setting a trap, that she is offering me coffee with feigned insouciance, that she wants to salvage the evening after a bad day at the office and needs my help.

As I take my cup, I let her know that she can count on me by giving her thigh a fleeting (and largely noncommittal) caress. We then launch into one of those banal and pointless conversations whose only aim is to pretend we are not animals, a preamble of words and smiles intended to civilize the imminent meeting of flesh. I think doves fluff up their crops. We, the guardians of Creation, are more refined. With calculated indifference, our bodies gradually gravitate toward each other, invading each other's space, clearly extending an invitation. I guess she is trying not to think of something else. To forget about that bastard boss of hers. Or how she will ask me to leave when all this is over. For my part, I'm attempting not to think about Virginia. Yet, in truth, what the two of us should have been thinking about is the cat.

It all happens incredibly fast. When our lips collide, we hear a terrifying screech. Next comes a flash of white lightning, almost too rapid to see. Before I can comprehend what has happened, the girl pulls away from me, howling with pain, covering her cheek with her hand. From between her splayed fingers spouts a torrent of blood. She flees to the bathroom and presses a towel to the claw marks scoring her cheek. I follow her, dumbfounded. Despite the impressive amount of blood, happily the wound does not appear to be too deep. The girl and the cat stare at each other, sizing each other up.

From that moment on, I have been the proud owner of a cat. The girl gave her to me, more or less. "Get this monster out of my home," she ordered, "or I won't be responsible for my actions." I opened the door and beckoned to the cat. She didn't even hesitate, but followed me straight to my apartment.

Now I spend most of the day in front of the television, with the cat curled up in a ball on my lap. Sometimes she licks my hands lovingly, and I absentmindedly stroke her hot, fluffy body. Most of the time, however, we simply stare at each other. We remain like this for hours on end. That's when I think I asked the wrong questions. I should have asked her very different ones, like *Who are you?* or *Who is looking at me through your eyes?*

I've no wish to think in terms of reincarnation because I've never believed in that sort of thing, but sometimes, at about my third or fourth drink, I can't resist opening the bedside drawer and unfolding yet again the obituary I came across in the newspaper the day after Virginia's disappearance, and which I cut out without knowing why, perhaps prompted by the coincidence of name and age. Now, when I consider the way the cat looks at me when I reread it, an absurd suspicion creeps into my mind. Perhaps the name is no coincidence. Perhaps, after all, Virginia died on her way home, hit by a car or felled by a heart attack. The way it occurred isn't important. What's important is that, as she said, once she had met me, she would never leave.

The Violinist on the Roof

It happened during a particularly hot summer, when everyone in Brooklyn seemed to be members of a secret society that conveyed its orders in code through white handkerchiefs raised to perspiring brows. Ice creams melted before you could find a shady spot in which to enjoy them, covering your hand in a milky mitten. Sleep was a slithery fish that could only be caught in ephemeral nets woven with the cigarettes we smoked hurriedly on fire escapes, to the sound of grown-ups making love and cats in heat in the lap of a sticky universe.

I like to think that I alone noticed the arrival of the violinist in all his splendor, that I alone recalled every detail of his appearance, as if I knew already that later on I would have to tell his story. That morning, I was leaning out of the window in the corridor on the second floor of our guesthouse, waiting for Tom and Bobby to overcome the resistance offered by the water hydrant so that I could go down and cool myself beneath the torrent of water that by then would be blessing the sidewalk. I would make up any old excuse for my lateness, and Tom and Bobby would look at each other in silence, but the heat would postpone their protests yet again. I had just turned thirteen, and yet it was already perfectly clear to me that life belonged to those who let other people do all the hard work, especially in summer. However, that day I was all for lending a hand, as the boys seemed to have lost their dexterity and the water was taking its time coming.

My eyes strayed down the street, along that strip of world I knew like the back of my hand, and from which I no longer expected any surprises. It was then that the violinist appeared from around the corner, erupting into our vanilla summer world with his slow gait, needle-thin frame, and radish-like paleness, encased in a suit as black as a coal miner's spittle. But what most struck me above all was the dark, mysterious violin case quivering at knee height like a baby whale stranded on a beach. The entire street stopped whatever it was doing then to watch him walk. Perhaps it was my feverish prayers that prevented the violinist from carrying on down the road, leaving us to our sad routine, my clenched fists and vows never to upset my mother again, which made his dusty Italian shoes come to a halt outside the entrance to our guesthouse.

He wrote only his surname on the register: *Peterson*, a centipede of letters that scarcely filled the blank space indicated by my father's chubby thumb, and which helped confirm his mysteriousness alongside the drearily precise names of the other guests. He had no other luggage than his violin, no suitcase that would give me an excuse to accompany him to his room. I had to be content to watch him mount the stairs, the silence of his gentle footfalls rousing the other guests as they nodded off in the easy chairs in the living room.

The grown-ups exchanged glances, and then went back to their newspapers; one of them, at most, devoting a moment to scratching his beard, eyes fixed on the stairs. Life is so full of mysteries that by the time you reach a certain age one more scarcely makes an impression. But I was thirteen, just old enough to make it my mission to solve the riddle posed by the violinist. What had brought him to our neighborhood? Was he a famous musician? Was he fleeing from something or hiding out? The novelty of this unusual character amid the dull patrons at our guesthouse seemed to me a unique opportunity to discover the world that lay beyond our neighborhood, away from the cluster of streets that encompassed my life. And it was clear to me that to see the violin, to hold it in my hands, could only enhance my reputation: in our neighborhood there were few chances of seeing let alone touching a violin, unless it was in Ed's store window. And so, during the days that followed, I loitered outside his room with the discipline of a sentry, as if the mere fact of meeting a violinist could salvage my childhood or imbue it with an aura of prestige.

For the first few days, the violinist only left his room to come down for the last serving of dinner, two hours after my bedtime. Mom told me he liked to eat alone, and that although only two other guests who were starting a shift ate at that hour, Peterson would sit at the farthest corner of the table. He seemed to have made it his own, she said, with his distant expression and his continuous cigarettes, like a presence so nervous it was calming. Mom liked to see that life wasn't only about accepting the ups and downs with a smile or a groan, and that it was possible to remain on the sidelines, content to observe without getting one's feet wet, refusing to choose because each choice implies a loss, spending a thousand nights and a thousand cigarettes waiting with tremendous patience for a favorable wind. Perhaps simply because she liked to contradict Dad, Mom insisted that Peterson wasn't a sad character, despite the way he looked in the far corner of the room, enveloped in plumes of smoke, but rather someone who had seen more things than were permitted to us, as if he had caught sight of his sister naked or something, and felt guilty about how much he had enjoyed it.

On day five of my stakeout, I was rewarded by a crack in the door and took full advantage of it. I entered the room, feigning that cautious timidity grown-ups expect from a child my age and that I would occasionally use as a passkey in situations like this. Peterson was sitting on his bed, a dying cigarette ember in his right hand, and on his lap one of the metal ashtrays Mom supplied to all the guests. Never had rooms in the guesthouse seemed to me so bleak. The violinist's posture, perched discreetly on the edge of a bed that showed only the creases made by his weight, as if since his arrival he hadn't bothered to explore the rest of the mattress, and the fact that his occupancy within those four walls boiled down to the violin case and his jacket hanging on a hook like a flayed bat, gave the scene an air of excruciating impermanence.

Hearing me enter, he gave me a blank stare through the cloud of smoke, which was neither a refusal nor an invitation. I approached his bed, brandishing my idiotic expression like a letter of safe conduct. Peterson didn't seem to mind me buzzing about his smoke-clouded figure as I tried to think of a clever way to start a conversation. Only when I mentioned his violin did he appear to notice me. He added his cigarette end to the water lily of butts he was creating in the ashtray and looked at me. It was a strange, drawn-out look, encircling me like a wet towel. I could feel his eyes close in on me with infinite calm, as though reconciled to have to do so, and then firmly take root in me, as if they might remain there forever. At that moment I wanted to believe that in the dispassionate drama of the violinist's life, I had ceased to be a prop and had become an important actor, someone with a presence onstage, which filled me with pride.

"A silent violin is the saddest thing in the world," he said at last, responding to a question that seemed distant to me now, as if it had been posed in another life or in a dream. His voice sounded terribly brittle and weak, like the crackle of a gramophone on a rainy day. He seemed accustomed to expressing himself only in these generous silences, never needing to compete with noises and shouts. "To contemplate a violin in its case," he went on, "is like being confronted with a dead child in its tiny casket, enveloped by death's passive beauty." He drew on his cigarette and looked away. "It is an object without a soul," he concluded, faced with my muteness. I observed the black case lying on the table with mounting curiosity.

"Play something, then," I said. Peterson turned his head slowly toward me with a look of annoyance. Then he squinted, pursing his lips in what seemed like a gesture of dismay. The bloodred evening filtered weakly through the narrow window, lending his angular face a conspiratorial, melodramatic air.

"I can't, I'm sorry," he apologized, "not yet." We remained silent for a while, observing each other through the smoke with a solemnity at once exaggerated and ridiculous, as though dazed by the mysterious turn the conversation had taken.

We didn't speak to each other again that morning. Although I was burning with curiosity, I decided to ignore all the questions in my head clamoring to be asked, and leave Peterson to his obscure reflections, playing the role of the patient confidante. I spent the next few days observing his comings and goings discreetly, acquainting myself with his routine, which resembled that of an insect trapped under a glass. Peterson would loiter for hours outside the entrance to the guesthouse, leaning indolently against a lamppost or patrolling the sidewalk, a twilight cigarette in one hand and the violin case in the other, as though waiting to catch a tram that never seemed to arrive. He paid scant attention to the other idle guests who would also wander about in the vicinity of the guesthouse; they must have seemed to him little more than souls in purgatory, and anyone attempting to start a conversation with that shy, gangly fellow would receive a slow exhalation of smoke in their faces for their pains. Like a stray dog absentmindedly sniffing at every corner, Peterson's gaze would wander along the street, then rise to the sky with a jolt, like a startled pigeon, only to drift to the ground once more with the meager indifference of a feather. But it was on the roof terrace that Peterson spent most of his time. He would drag a chair up there, puff away on his cigarettes, always with the violin case at his feet, like an old dog dozing on his shoes. Almost every day without fail, when night began to sweep away the last rays of evening, Peterson would come down to the tiny parlor and with a doleful expression go over to the telephone. There he would conduct a brief conversation, composed of barely whispered grunts and solemn nods, from which he emerged still more dispirited.

My tasks permitting, I would try to follow him about silently, to ensure that I was the first person his distracted gaze alighted upon when it came back to reality in search of a reference point. Whenever I saw Mom carrying a basket of wet laundry I would snatch it from her with an eagerness she probably mistook for admirable kindness. I would hurry upstairs, leaving in my wake a trail of droplets and clothes pegs, overjoyed at being able to assail the violinist in such a discreet manner. After I had hung up the washing, I would hang around on the roof and then approach Peterson on the pretext of cadging a cigarette. I would remain by his side, helping him to observe the orange sunset spreading before us.

This was when I discovered that in common with everyone, save perhaps for the violinist himself, my patience had its limits. One afternoon, weary of his silence, and having learned by heart all the color changes in the day before it embraces night, I ventured to resume our unfinished conversation.

"Why do you never play your violin?" I asked him. Peterson looked at me lengthily, his eyes reflecting his habitual caution and fatigue. But he just ignored my question and went on smoking, ruthlessly crushing my frail dreams of friendship. However, he did reply to it the following afternoon, after calling me over.

I was on my way downstairs, carrying the empty basket, an exaggeratedly sullen expression on my face, the last chance for a plan that was starting to look as if it had backfired. His sudden change of attitude took me by surprise. Peterson appeared to regret the indifference he had shown me the day before; he made me sit down facing him and produced the first smile I had ever seen from him, a touchingly awkward puckering of his lips, the smile of a novice clown who has overdone the makeup. Maybe, after all, he needed a friend as well, someone who could be like an oasis on that solitary journey he had decided to make, someone on whom he could test out his words to make sure they hadn't become defunct through lack of use. Then, in a mysterious voice, he told me about his apprenticeship as a violinist, about his many years of practice, of almost religious dedication to that proud, sensual instrument whose exquisite wooden contours had supplanted during his teenage years the warm curves his fingers desired.

With an extraordinary series of demonstrative gestures and dramatic inhalations, he recounted the story of his long, lonely nights hammering out the raw material of his talent—a talent that the elderly teacher he'd had as a child, whose name he couldn't remember, had emphasized to his mother—until finally his fingers had achieved a more-than-remarkable dexterity. But that wasn't all; it remained to be seen whether he possessed true genius or not, whether there was the slightest possibility of him achieving the fantasies that were inevitably starting to invade his thoughts. To perfect his art, he chose La Campanella by the esteemed Paganini, a Genoese composer whom it was rumored had made a pact with the devil. For years he practiced tirelessly, with much anguish, approaching his goal with such disheartening slowness that he feared he would never reach it. And then one evening, while he was playing without much conviction, he was astonished to discover in the quavering silence that followed, that he had managed to play the much-practiced piece to perfection. Having once achieved this miracle, a sort of superstition had prevented him from ever playing it again, possibly out of fear of discovering that his magnificent performance owed more to chance than to his imaginary ability. That troubling notion had caused him to place the violin back in its case, hoping to conserve the sublime melody intact in its strings, as one might hold a dove in one's hands, preserving its energy, putting off the sky, delaying its flight until the right moment.

And that moment was about to arrive, he assured me. In the penthouse apartment of the building opposite the guesthouse lived Paolo Volpi. He was a wealthy entrepreneur, who in addition to his many businesses owned a well-known Broadway theater. People in the neighborhood didn't talk about him much, and the only thing I knew about Don Paolo was that he liked good food, expensive cigars, and chorus girls. And that he must have oodles of money, because he had a gold tooth and was always traveling. Only very occasionally would I bump into his rotund figure out in the street, greeting storekeepers with his beaming smile, like a president taking the nation's pulse. The shutters on his windows remained closed for most of the year, and his roof terrace exhibited unabashed a wilted row of blighted pot plants. It was toward this roof terrace that Peterson's longing gaze would stray, for Don Paolo, the violinist informed me, possessed one of the most discerning ears on the East Coast. It was little wonder, then, that, according to the critics, he had formed the only orchestra capable of competing with a choir of angels. Peterson's dream was to join that prodigious orchestra, and yet he had never managed to get an audition. This was what had brought him to our neighborhood. This was the reason why he was forced to spend hours on the roof, smoking with a tragic air amid mangy cats and wet laundry. This was the reason why he was here, waiting at the ready with his violin on our roof, eyes fixed on Don Paolo's terrace, fingers itching with a terrible desire to play, to climb back on that bucking bronco that was Paganini's piece.

"When he appears, I shall open the case," he confided, "I swear." He drew on his cigarette and ended his tale with a tremulous smile that looked more like an anguished grimace.

I smiled too, captivated, and yet also satisfied. Peterson's story had exceeded my expectations. I imagined that the violinist was dragging around behind him a beautiful, mysterious past, folded like a peacock's tail—a past he had just revealed to me alone, fanning out its splendid array of colors. I imagined him growing up as a child with his violin, cut off from life in his goldfish bowl of notes and scores, like a moth hypnotized by shimmering sequins, imprisoned in a storybook fate whose ending was about to take place on my roof terrace. I was determined to witness the denouement, as if my life depended on it: Peterson, standing silhouetted against the bloodred sunset, the sweep of rooftops, his violin tucked beneath his chin, standing erect, the slumbering melody sliding toward Don Paulo's ears, surprising him as he watered his plants. My excited expression seemed to please Peterson, and his smile became less rigid, more relaxed.

"No one must know about this, okay?" he added. "It'll be our secret." I nodded, thrilled at this request, which only gave more weight to his story, and at the gentle connivance with which he had offered me a slice of his soul, like a traveler sharing his bread with anyone who came near his fire. He

ventured to complete the fraternal scene by reaching out his
hand to muss up my hair, a gesture he probably didn't make
very often, judging by the clumsy way he performed it, his
nimble right hand like a smooth tarantula tangled in my curls.
Then he returned his gaze to the sunset, which was making
the sky go as red as a chilblain. I studied the back of his neck,
the motion of his cigarette, the erratic scrawl of smoke, and
a sensation very like affection welled up inside me. Before
the violinist arrived, my heart had been incapable of such a
refined feeling, of containing all together pity, admiration,
sorrow, and pride.

"Who is it you call every afternoon?' I asked, eager to fit
that piece into the intriguing puzzle of his past. I saw the hand
that was holding his cigarette tense all of a sudden, just for a
few seconds, before resuming its elegant ascension to his lips.
Three slow inhalations brought a response.

"Evelyn," he said, without turning. "I call Evelyn." And there
was no need for him to say more. The anguished tone with
which he uttered her name was enough for me to picture a
pretty, slender woman, her hair styled like a movie actress,
waiting for him in a house that seemed to grow smaller every
day without his presence, wondering how long it was going
to take for his dream to become a reality, how long she would
be able to survive with nothing but his increasingly hoarse
voice over the telephone. Evelyn and her blue eyes behind
the shutters. Evelyn looking out on a street veiled with rain.
Evelyn imagining that she sees silhouettes on afternoons that

drag on forever. Evelyn, who no longer knows how to ration the kisses and caresses she conserves in her memory. Evelyn, the final brushstroke that completes the beautiful picture.

The next morning, Mom sent me on various errands, which took me virtually to the outer reaches of the neighborhood. I hadn't stopped relishing the violinist's story during the night, marveling at the romanticism of those images imprinted on my imagination. On my way home, I decided to stop by Ed's music store, because now more than ever I needed to see a violin, to have a more precise idea of the instrument that so implacably ruled Peterson's life. There were two in the window, dangling like fish in a smokehouse. And yet, despite their undeniable beauty, the harmony of those contours, like a gazelle preparing to leap, I could see them only as dead things, sad, soulless objects, which without the skilled hands to give them meaning were no more than a whimsical fusion of wood and metal.

When I returned to the guesthouse, this is what I wanted to tell Peterson. Dad was behind the counter, immersed in the sports section of the morning paper; he was one of those grown-ups who give more importance to baseball heroes than to the people in their own lives. There was no sign of the violinist in the parlor, so I assumed I would find him in his room. I ran upstairs and into the corridor. Peterson's door was closed, which struck me as odd, because he had recently started to leave it ajar to prevent the accumulation of cigarette smoke becoming a dense fog. Maybe he was already on the roof. I was raising my hand to call out to see if that was the case, when his door opened from the inside. Mom glanced at me briefly as if she didn't recognize me. I smiled at her, but my smile soon faded when I realized that she wasn't returning my gesture, but was simply staring at me, her mouth set in a hard line, a suspicious look in her eyes. This intense scrutiny alarmed me. Not knowing what else to do, I held her gaze until, finally, with considerable effort, her lips curved into a smile, aimed at reassuring which one of us I wasn't sure. I noticed she was holding a pile of tin ashtrays. Then she stroked my head and moved on to the next room to continue her task, still glancing at me over her shoulder with that strange expression.

Peterson was in his room, smoking with his usual indolence over by the window. Smoke rings shaped like seahorses rose from his lips. I had to clear my throat to get him to notice me. He seemed to give a start when he saw me. He smiled to himself, nodded, then finally approached me terribly slowly, as if he was walking on a raft. He placed his right hand on my shoulder. He exuded a smell both strong and mild, as if he'd been sleeping on a bed of chrysanthemums.

"Come on, I'll buy you an ice cream," he said.

Rody's was the best ice cream parlor in the neighborhood, and it was on our street. We bought two large chocolate ice creams and sat down to eat them on the sidewalk outside the guesthouse.

The afternoon was slowly coming into its own, the temperature was rising, the air was still, and the world looked like a photograph of itself. I became absorbed in my ice cream, as soon as I saw the first trickles running down the cone like dried blood. This was the first time in my life that I'd had a large cone, and I wasn't about to waste it. I was hoping Tom and Bobby might show up, drawn by the peculiar scent of satisfied desires, to act as dumb witnesses to my pleasure, their envy immortalizing the eternity of chocolate. Where's the fun in a large ice cream if there's no one to see you enjoying it?

It was then that Peterson leaped to his feet. I looked at him, startled. He was visibly distressed, eyes open wide, lips covered with terror and chocolate. I followed his gaze to Don Paolo's roof garden. There he was, leaning on the handrail, contemplating the street with that mixture of affection and indolence of someone who has escaped hell but allows himself an occasional visit. His thinning hair was disheveled, his belly encased in a sleeveless vest, with a woolly tuft escaping at his midriff. Peterson turned toward me, thrust his ice cream into my hand, and ran into the guesthouse.

I was too slow to respond, to realize that the denouement of the story that had me in its grip was about to take place. Peterson was rushing to get his violin, and I had to go after him if I wanted a ringside seat. I looked at the two chocolate ice creams glistening in my hands like trophies. I looked at the rickety trash can, annoyingly close on my left. Then I looked up at Don Paolo's roof garden and saw him idly swatting a fly from his face. I looked again at the two half-melted scepters in my hands. I cursed and threw them in the trash, relieved in the end that Tom and Bobby weren't there, for they would have regarded my action as a sacrilege akin to urinating in a chalice.

Dad watched with relative indifference as I shot across the hallway, immune to the caprices of his son, which he puzzled over as he might a crossword. I devoured the stairs in avid leaps and dashed along the corridor, dizzy with anticipation before the imminent finale, my chocolate-smeared fingers leaving a trail of black moth marks on the walls that would later baffle Mom. As I raced past Peterson's room, I peered inside to make sure my suspicions were correct and that the case was no longer on the table. I let out a grunt of frustration. The violinist had a good head start over me. And I knew that if the strains of the violin finally being played on the rooftop were to reach me at that moment I would have no choice but to fall to my knees in the middle of the corridor and shed tears of despair. I mounted the stairs to the roof terrace, my heart pounding from the excitement and the effort, leaping over steps between gasps, overwhelmed by a sinking feeling. In fact, I would have preferred the story to reach its conclusion a couple of days later, long enough at least for me to savor the magnificent climax, to prepare myself for an ending, which, however beautiful, was the final curtain. Afterward, Peterson would leave, victorious or defeated, but he would leave. Nothing would keep him on our roof.

I reached the terrace just in time to see Peterson slam down the lid of his violin case with a dispirited gesture, to hear the terrible creak of the clasps. I ran over to him, leaned over the handrail, gasping for breath, and searched for Don Paolo, but his terrace was empty. Peterson had arrived too late. While he was fetching his violin, Don Paolo had gone back inside, possibly tired of the flies, possibly even disgusted by his neighbors' comings and goings, the sad way they dragged themselves through life, gnawing timidly at the world. Beside me, rigid as a totem pole, Peterson contemplated the deserted roof terrace, scarcely containing his anger, as if he couldn't quite believe this had happened. He remained like that a long while, with no energy or desire for a cigarette, his left hand hovering above the lid of the case. I stood beside him, glancing by turns at Don Paolo's roof terrace, even though it was becoming more obvious by the minute that he wouldn't return, at the case containing that elusive violin, and at Peterson, startled by the feverish glint in his eyes, the harsh curl of his lips. I saw his face darken. I saw the afternoon fade in his hair, die slowly in his eyes. Before I knew it, night had fallen. I thrust my hands in my pockets and went downstairs to dinner knowing that I would only play with my food, that I would go to bed unable to rid myself of the bitter taste that lost opportunities leave in the mouth.

"You look more wilted than Mrs. Flannery's lettuces," my mother said to me the next morning, when she saw me slumped over the counter. About time too: I had been silently trying to catch her attention all morning, scowling in the corner, adopting dejected postures in her line of sight. I needed to speak with her, to find out whether with her scalpel-like comprehension she could lance the boil of anxiety that had grown in me overnight, once the previous afternoon's events had settled in my head and I was able to go over them with the terrible lucidity insomnia bestows upon us. I had reached the conclusion that this was the first time, the only time, Peterson had gone out without his violin, and I realized with a pang of anguish that I was ultimately to blame for this omission. Because, while the ice cream had been his idea, it was my presence in his room that had brought it about. There was no doubt in my mind that if I hadn't appeared, the violinist would have gone up to the roof with his violin, the way he always did, or maybe he would have gone out. In any event, he would have taken the case with him. The aim of my confession was to rid myself of guilt, or at least to assuage it, even though I would feel fresh guilt at betraying Peterson by letting my mother in on our secret. But I considered this a harmless exchange, from which I hoped to come out better off.

Mom listened to my tale, a smile playing on her lips, while every so often Dad glanced up from his paper, irritated, as if he couldn't understand what possible significance this could have when one of the best third basemen of the New York Yankees had broken a leg.

"Don't torment yourself, sweetie—sometimes things turn out one way and not another," she tried to reassure me. "Besides, I'm sure Don Paolo won't be going just yet. You wait and see, Peterson will soon have another chance, and he'll seize it."

Talking to Mom reassured me somewhat, but that day I didn't dare go near Peterson, who even brought his case with him down to dinner, as though he too acknowledged my guilt and was trying to reproach me. I watched him pacing up and down the sidewalk, eyes fixed on Don Paolo's terrace, smoking on the roof, the black violin case on his knees, and more dejected than ever when he called Evelyn. I would have spent the whole of the next day doing the same thing, if my father hadn't asked me around midday to bring the violinist down to reception. I climbed the stairs grudgingly. On top of everything else, I was now forced to break the silence that had descended between us with more bad news, because it was obvious that Dad didn't wish to see Peterson in reception to discuss music. In all likelihood, Peterson owed several days' rent. This setback would doubtless finish him off. I found him in his room, smoking over by the window, and I delivered the message in a faint voice, too afraid to look at him. Peterson nodded reluctantly, picked up the violin case, and followed me downstairs.

Neither of us expected to encounter Don Paolo's radiant smile in reception. Dad stood next to him, also smiling, shamelessly revealing his crooked, yellow teeth like a sad parody of Don Paolo's gesture. I could see Mom watching silently in the background. Don Paulo was dressed in an elegant white suit, hair glistening with brilliantine, the pudgy fingers of his right hand wrapped around a cigar, whose rich aroma would linger in the hallway for days.

"This is the young fellow, Don Paolo," Dad announced. Don Paolo stepped forward, examining the violinist from head to toe, studying his angular face and his threadbare black jacket, and finally coming to rest on the case he was holding in his pale hand. Then he looked straight at Peterson, whose bewildered eyes met his.

"So, you want to join my orchestra," he said. Peterson turned white. Don Paolo's lips curved in an amused smile. His gold tooth seized the opportunity to glint like a stiletto.

"Everything is ready," a voice reached them from the parlor. My father gave a contented nod and, linking arms with Don Paolo, led him toward the room.

A couple of other guests had arranged the armchairs in the parlor into an improvised auditorium. With dramatic solemnity, Dad invited the violinist to sit down on the chair that presided over the room while the rest of us hurriedly took up the other seats, forming an expectant and rather noisy huddle. But the whispers ceased when Don Paolo sliced the air with an authoritative wave of his hand, initiating that deep, reverential silence that fills holy places. I observed the hushed company, the familiar faces now curiosity-stricken, yet solemn as Roman busts. Apart from the two guests who had moved the furniture, a few loafers had wandered in off the street. Mom had also joined the audience, although she preferred to watch from the hallway. When Dad saw her, his raggedy smile broadened.

Ensconced in his chair, Don Paolo contemplated the violinist, beaming as if it were his daughter's wedding day.

From his makeshift seat of honor, Peterson observed us, intimidated, lips pursed, eyes full of misgiving. Events had gone way beyond his control. I watched him take a deep breath as he tried to collect himself, to accept as true this crazy situation, which he saw as utterly insane, to stop the violin case dancing on his cicada knees. I sat back in my chair, also trying desperately to control my nerves. Although not how I'd imagined it, I was about to witness the denouement of Peterson's story, the finale of his electrifying feat. I was going to see his violin, hear his music, take part in his dream. Once he had managed to absorb what was taking place, Peterson recovered a degree of poise and held Don Paolo's scrutinizing gaze for a long time.

I was astonished at the incongruous rage congealing in his eyes, the intense anger which soon began to radiate from his sockets. I imagined he found it unpleasant to discover that, despite its chaotic appearance, the world was a terribly orderly place that could be divided into two distinct groups: those who dreamed and those who made dreams happen. Don Paolo held his furious gaze without batting an eyelid, sucking lazily on his cigar, amplifying his smile so that his lips seemed to twist into a disturbing, even menacing grimace. He appeared to enjoy the discomfort of the violinist, an insect writhing beneath the glare of his magnifying glass. This staring contest seemed to have gone on for an eternity, when Don Paolo pointed his eyes at the case and invited Peterson to proceed with a polite tilt of his head that seemed to infuriate the violinist even more. With a mixture of loathing and trepidation, Peterson looked down at the case in his lap; then he looked again at Don Paolo's defiant smile, his shiny gold teeth, before resting his eyes once more on the case. Mournfully, his pale fingers caressed the catches, even as his face took on an appearance of profound determination. Then, just as we were all expecting the lid of the case to spring open, Peterson leaped from his chair, clasped hold of the case, and hurried out of the room, elbowing aside the astonished guests who were blocking the exit.

The violinist's unexpected flight caused a chorus of murmurs before Don Paolo's disconcerting laugh rang out like a shot. He seemed to be the only one who wasn't surprised at Peterson's departure. Crammed into his armchair, he dissolved in a hoarse, jarring guffaw, fiendish in its intensity. I took advantage of the general confusion to slip out of the room and into the street. In the distance, I could see the violinist, who stood out like a capital letter among the other pedestrians. I watched him disappear for good down the street as if someone were extracting my spleen. This was the end, the final act of an unfinished story.

Peterson didn't have the courage to fulfill his dream, and now all his sacrifices seemed painfully in vain. Perhaps the icy disdain, the savage hatred I had seen explode in his eyes was directed only at himself, for when the moment of truth arrived, he had realized he was a coward, diminished, incapable of taking the leap, of confronting the possible failure that would make his life hollow, annihilate his existence in one fell swoop. I imagined him framed in Evelyn's window like a wounded shadow, dragging the violin case along the ground, broken, stooped, drunk perhaps, secretly glad that the rain was concealing his tears. I shook my head. The scene was too painful. I decided not to judge him. I refused to think of him as a coward. Perhaps instead of destroying him, this ordeal would make him stronger. Evelyn would soothe him with her caresses, would lighten his load with her unwavering support. And maybe one day, Peterson would find the courage to settle his fate, to face Don Paolo with a beaming smile, open the case, and take out his violin, for better or worse.

"He can't be very good," I heard my father say with his bucktoothed laugh in the parlor.

"I'm sure you're right," Don Paulo agreed, his laughter beginning to slacken. "I'm sure you're right."

That afternoon I went up to the roof terrace and smoked a cigarette as a tribute to the violinist while the sky became permeated with the usual colors.

After Peterson's departure, the days lost their sparkle. They returned to normal, flowing monotonously and predictably, with their smattering of the same pranks performed a thousand times, the same lurid banter exchanged a thousand times, of large chocolate ice creams once again beyond reach. Sometimes, when dusk began to infiltrate the sky, I would meet with Tom and Bobby on the roof terrace and tell them the story of the violinist. I spoke to them of his mysterious gaze, his black suit, his dying cigarettes, his life devoted to the violin, and, although here I was obliged to embellish, of the beautiful instrument slumbering in its case, Paganini's refrain crackling on its strings, of its frailty, its weightlessness, how it seemed it might crumble in my hands. But, since Bobby kept insisting that, according to his father, the only orchestra in Don Paolo's dive was a mediocre jazz band, we grew bored of the subject, and ended up talking about baseball and Mrs. Flannery's daughter, who it was rumored had begun wearing a bra that summer. I thought no more about the violinist until a few months later, when we heard that Don Paolo had died. Death had surprised him as he left his theater, piercing his skull in the form of a bullet someone had fired from a rooftop.

"It was bound to happen sooner or later. People like that never die in their beds," my mother remarked when she found out, as if Don Paolo had been born with that bullet clasped in his tiny closed fist. Comments like my mother's were widespread. Even so, for two days, everyone in the neighborhood mourned Don Paulo. I mourned for Peterson, who now would never be able to turn his dream into reality.

The Man behind the Curtain

fell in love with Marta when, on one of our first dates, I heard her swear she'd never experienced that well-known sensation of entering somewhere for the first time and feeling she had been there before. I remember she emphasized the unusual nature of her confession with a wave of the arm that ended up spilling her coffee over the nightstand, and I stared at her, suddenly spellbound, as she tried to repair the damage by soaking tissues in the pool of coffee. Since I too had never felt that prickling in the nape of the neck that affects others when they cross certain thresholds, I felt a sudden onrush of affection for this skinny girl I had been courting in a lackluster way for some time. This was strong enough to intertwine our lives as poor creatures immune to this kind of déjà vu. A more passionate kiss than usual sealed her revelation. And as the days went by, we realized that neither of us had any wish to look for anything else, that we were both content with this bonanza that was so akin to boredom. As a result, in front of an altar decked out with spikenards and besieged by a mob of relatives who had appeared out of the most remote hiding places, we decided to close the file on the dark days of the past when we had treated love in the same way as children treat electric sockets. And it was now, our backs bent from seven years of conjugal routine that had produced a fast-growing daughter and a grandmother on her way to the scrap heap, that all of a sudden, the old flame was rekindled, without either of us wishing it. The reason was none other than our search for a new roof to shelter under, because when I took my eyes off the swaying hips of the girl from the real estate agency to actually look at the spacious apartment she was showing us, I felt a prickling at the back of my neck that made me turn toward Marta. I could tell from her eyes that she also had the impression of having been there before.

There was no doubt it was the home of our dreams. It had an immense living room, light and airy bedrooms, and two bathrooms, which meant we would be able to avoid family life being suspended in a painful impasse whenever Grandma decided to barricade herself in one of them. The only thing that detracted from it being our dreamed-of den was the presence of the man behind the curtain.

"Who is he?" Marta wanted to know.

The girl from the real estate agency simply shrugged. There wasn't much she could tell us. She didn't know his name or the reason why he was there, hidden or waiting for heaven knows what. The only thing she could say was that the man behind the curtain came with the apartment, that he was, as it were, part of the furniture. If we eventually decided to rent it, he came included in the price, and if, at some point, we decided to move, we also had to hand the apartment over with him inside. That was how it had always been, according to the agreement the first owner had established with the agency.

After informing us of these peculiar conditions, she left Marta and me on our own to make up our minds in private. Of all the ones we had seen, this apartment came closest to satisfying us. And yet, although we had moved several times in the course of our marriage, we had never lived with an unknown presence behind the living room curtain. Would we get used to it? The agent had told us that, according to previous tenants, it didn't make much difference, because the man behind the curtain was very reserved by nature and it took only a few days for them to forget he was there. Marta seemed to study closely the tips of the shoes poking out from the curtain hem. When she glanced toward me again, I understood that for her the presence of an intruder was no obstacle to our renting the place, and so I dipped my head meekly to show my agreement. After all, it was a relief to discover that the apartment wasn't haunted, as we had feared from the rumors circulating in the neighborhood.

We moved in at once. Apart from converting one of the bedrooms into a study for Marta and moving some of the furniture around, we made hardly any changes. However, our family life took some time to return to normal. I never learned whether the man behind the curtain regarded our arrival as an invasion of his territory or a welcome distraction from his solitude. In fact, we didn't notice any modification in his behavior because, as the girl from the real estate agency had informed us, he remained engrossed in his silent vigil, apparently indifferent to the domestic whirlwind all round him. He would move his head timidly in response to the questions my daughter, Eva, put to him—she was the only one who made an effort to be friendly toward that strange stowaway in our routine. Otherwise, it was only those of us who crossed the living room in the early hours to get a glass of water that had the privilege of hearing sounds coming from behind the curtain, almost always an unintelligible word mingled with the calm breathing of sleep. But it was precisely this circumspect attitude, the fact that we didn't have the slightest idea what he thought about our conduct, that we found most difficult to accept. For some time, it obliged us to avoid swearing or making polite conversation, and to dress up our actions with a grotesque solemnity, implausible ethics. Fortunately, we soon stopped feeling inhibited by his presence, and our attitudes went back to their abandoned simplicity, their unfussy vulgarity. It soon ceased to bother me that Marta strolled around the living room dressed only in the towel from her shower. I even encouraged her to do so, because I wanted to convey to our intruder by this show of tolerance that I considered him a eunuch in all senses of the word, a being to whose vegetative state one could freely abandon oneself to one's worst vices or even commit murders in the sure knowledge that one was in the most complete intimacy. To me, he was nobody, almost nothing at all; at most, a little animal with no awareness that I occasionally allowed Eva to offer a bowl of milk or my razor.

Days went by and turned into years without the mystery of his being there ceasing to intrigue us. Each family member drew their own conclusions about the man behind the curtain. Grandma, who rarely considered us worthy of sharing her lengthy meditations with, startled us at supper one evening by issuing a gloomy warning that the presence behind the curtain was no less than death himself. I supposed that this suggestion of hers was due to the repeated surgical pillaging, gouging, and sewing up she had been subjected to throughout the previous decade, useless temporary repairs that led her to imagine that any moment now a hooded figure bearing a scythe would appear from behind the curtain, place the scaly sparrow of a hand on her shoulder, and declare: *Come, Dolores, say farewell to this bunch of ingrates—there's nothing left for you here.* And she would get to her feet meekly and permit herself to be led behind the curtain without any parting wave of the hand or, at most, a brief attempt to caress her granddaughter's head. But not a word of thanks to her daughter, still less to her daughter's unfortunate husband, who time and again threatened her with the old people's home whenever, in the midst of a meal, she triumphantly yielded to the mortifying demands of her intestines. For her part, my daughter Eva, by now submerged in the hormonal cataclysm of adolescence, soon stopped considering the man behind the curtain as an exotic pet to be fed and began to look at him in a different way, to study with a mixture of curiosity and hope the hominid specimen vaguely outlined by the drape. Eva grew up fascinated by the curtain, dreaming of the outline it projected, while her girlfriends fantasized about actors of the day, even though both of them were irredeemably headed for the pedestrian reality of the boys in adjacent desks. It took only a couple of Eva's failed dates with her schoolmates for me to realize that Eva would never be happy with a man, that something within her would inevitably spoil her relationships at the least sign of them continuing, that no male, however perfect he was, would ever be able to rival the person hidden behind the curtain, that anonymous silhouette onto which she had projected all her fantasies. Of all the family, it was Marta's attitude that was closest to mine. The man behind the curtain did not seem to give her pause for thought in any way: she simply accepted his presence there with the same forced smile that you adopt to receive those ghastly wedding gifts you know are unavoidable.

But conjectures about the intentions of the man behind the curtain were not monopolized by our family. My work colleague Soriano also allowed himself an opinion on the subject during our coffee breaks. Although, thanks to his prosaic nature, his considerations never ventured into the realm of philosophy, but remained grounded in the sexual arena, the only one that appeared to interest him. Didn't two and two make four? Didn't Marta work at home, stuck in her study while a total stranger lurked in the living room? How many hours could she translate Milton without becoming weary, without having a break for a drink of water or a shower, or, why not, to fornicate wildly with the man behind the curtain? How was it possible that I had never stopped to consider the obvious, that while I was busy at work this stranger had the run of my domain, and could appropriate what was mine, convert my home sweet home into a garden of lust? Soriano was a poor guy who was constantly leaving work to run the ridiculous errands his wife loaded him with, and so his insinuations didn't worry me in the slightest. It wasn't that I had a blind faith in Marta, but because I was incapable of imagining the man behind the curtain emerging from a years-long paralysis, the way the warriors of ancient Greece had poured out of the Trojan horse. Besides, Grandma was there, like a kind of drooling censor whose mere presence was enough to cool the most passionate libido. It was when we had to hospitalize her for the umpteenth time that the seed Soriano had tried so hard to plant in my mind began suddenly to sprout, as a result of the answer my wife gave when I asked how long her mother was going to be in the clinic for. "Forever, I hope," she muttered with a soft, sleepy pursing of the lips that was not hard to interpret as a smile of secret satisfaction. Under Soriano's influence, it seemed to me this comment could express both Marta's wish to see the family freed of the troublesome burden as the certainty that this made it open season for licentiousness.

One night, weary of struggling to get to sleep because of
these baseless suspicions, I got out of bed and went into the
living room, determined to speak for the first time to the
man behind the curtain. He was sleeping peacefully, even
snoring quite tunefully with the kind of methodical hum of
household appliances. Placing a chair directly in front of him,
I asked straight out if he was having an affair with my wife. It
took him a while to wake up and realize that the head of the
family he had attached himself to with such impunity was
addressing him. I heard him clearing his throat noisily, and
shortly afterward, out of the curtain came a friendly, melodic
little voice. After giving me an excessively polite greeting, he
informed me that he had not so much as noticed my wife, even
though he was sure that she must be as attractive as I was.
Then, as though feeling responsible for the ensuing silence,
he made a timid attempt to break it, adding a few details to
the topic, and when he discovered I was making no attempt
to restrain him, he continued with a tale that soon took on a
confidential note.

He explained that there was no longer any room for love
in his heart. He only had eyes for one woman—the one whose
return he was waiting for behind the curtain. He had fallen
in love at first sight with Virtudes almost seventy years ago,
and his love was requited, but life had led them to meet three
years too late, the length of time she had been married to a
man for whom she felt nothing more than a calm affection
that was a pale shadow of the passion burning inside her

whenever she was in the presence of our stranger. In those days, it wasn't considered the thing to do to shuffle the cards you were dealt by life, and so they could only assuage the fever coursing through their veins by having recourse to the obscure mechanics of furtive meetings that only served to make them feel ashamed of themselves. During one of these encounters, the husband's key turned in the lock sooner than expected, and the love of his life obliged him to hide behind the curtain. From there, he witnessed their re-encounter, and the slow passage of the following hours that soon turned into days and then months, wishing only for the moment when she finally confronted her feelings and resolved to pull back the drape and wipe the frost from his lips. This moment never arrived. His eyes clouded by tears, he had watched her dreaming on the sofa as the leaves on the trees outside turned yellow, stroll around the apartment while he was comforted by the more-than-welcome heat from the stove, but on those nights when his rival stretched out his arms in response to the effervescence of spring, the moans of his beloved told him she had been brought up on edifying biographies that meant she rejected any kind of outrage and accepted that life had an unalterable order, like the queues in a butcher's shop. Even so, he did not give up, and remained behind the curtain, confident that if not her, then at least life, with its swings and roundabouts, would take it upon itself to draw back the drape separating them. It seemed on the point of doing so when Virtudes's husband disappeared. She came back from an outing with her female friends to discover he was not at home. She waited up for him, but he did not come back either that night or those that followed, so that Virtudes realized her husband must finally have noticed the man behind the curtain and been unable to carry on with what he supposed was nothing more than a farce. At that point, the man behind the curtain believed that there was no longer any reason for her not to pull back the drape and for them at last to live happily ever after. And yet, convinced that no happiness could be built on another person's suffering, Virtudes had in fact decided to move, and to rent out the apartment as soon as she found the strength or the dignity to renounce the love waiting behind the curtain for her.

Despite this, my anonymous interlocutor still felt that having known Virtudes had been the best thing that had ever happened to him, even though it had condemned him to this statuesque existence in which only the regular beat of his heart reminded him he had not died. Every cloud has a silver lining, and he had been able to find tiny pleasures in his voluntary marginalization. Over time, the curtain had exceeded its role as a hiding place and become a sort of privileged observatory, not only of other people's joys and misfortunes but also of the changes in the world, as he heard from the voice of the television. By dint of observing without interfering, like a diffident God, he had learned that life was nothing more than a joke in bad taste, a riddle that had to be solved through decisions that always involved losing, and for this at least he had to be thankful. While his status as a household totem pole had deprived him of certain pleasures, at the same time it had spared him a lot of remorse and frustration.

However, his explanation did not dispel my suspicions. All I had to do was pay close attention to Marta's behavior to detect at least a dozen clues of a joyous, continuing betrayal. The unconcerned way in which she paraded her nakedness, for example, rather than demonstrating her disdain for the virility of our intruder, began to seem to me the corollary of a lover's intimacy. And, although the fellow had appeared sincere, it was not unlikely that Marta, despite the lack of imagination she showed in bed with me, knew enough tricks of the trade for the man behind the curtain's passivity not to present any problem. Whatever the truth, the fact was that my flammable mistrust ended up collapsing the fragile scaffolding holding up our marriage. Both of us gave up on any rescue mission and turned with satisfaction to the slow invasion of the devouring moths.

I had the feeling that my entire life was a lie. Not only did places I had never been to start to seem familiar to me, but, sunk in a kind of numbness toward the world, anything that happened each day appeared to me predictable, a stupid repetition. I let the years slip by in this state of lethargy, as they solved—at an excruciatingly slow pace that even so was not without its suspense—the equation of my existence and that of my family. The passage of time also revealed that none of the members of our family had been right in our calculations

about the man behind the curtain. Following a record of boy-
friends that when it was reeled off sounded like the lineup of
a football team, Eva realized in the end that Prince Charmings
only exist behind curtains, and that the closest she could
come to that was to imbibe each man's moment of innocence,
those fleeting moments of naivety when the monster played
with the little girl without knowing he could drown her in
the lake with his own hands. She emigrated abroad, to some
countryside or other with an unpronounceable name, possibly because she had exhausted the purity of all the males
in Spain. From there she wrote me the lengthy letters of an
old maid with cats, leaving me to read between the lines
that she was miserably happy. As for Grandma, she died in
a hospital, without the intervention of the man behind the
curtain, fading away with stoic dignity during my turn to visit
her. I imagine she passed somewhat disgruntled that she had
to perform the ceremony of her dying to the least interested
spectator of her entourage. When I went home to give Marta
the news, I found her astride Soriano and understood that I
too had been mistaken, and that the man behind the curtain
was not my wife's lover.

After that evening, Marta and I had nothing to discuss apart
from how long we would allow each other to find somewhere
to live before we gave up the apartment we had shared. She
soon found a loft in the center where Soriano, after shrugging
his shoulders at me, went every morning to run his wife's
errands. I decided to stay on in the apartment until the real

estate agency began to show it. I left my packed suitcases next to the curtain. They demonstrated an appetite for travel I could not share, as no destination seemed to me sufficiently distant for me to get far enough away from myself.

On the morning the agency advised me that the first clients would be appearing that afternoon, I placed the chair in front of the man behind the curtain and read him the last letter I had received from Eva. In it she spoke, inevitably, about him: this was the topic that all the previous ones had ended up being about as well. In this one, however, she didn't speculate about his looks or his meaning in our lives, as she often liked to do in complex philosophical arguments, but informed me that, after many attempts, she had succeeded in locating Virtudes, the owner of the apartment. She lived alone, far from the hustle and bustle of the world, in a mansion with Gothic touches. Eva had gone there to see her, and found an impossibly young woman, a beautiful girl of no more than twenty, who wore her hair and clothes like a heroine of the silent cinema. Eva had to use all of her powers of persuasion for the woman to finally lay bare her soul and, after the fourth cup of tea beneath the crumbling vine trellis, reveal that it was the fact that she had not pulled back the curtain, not yielded to the love that chance had offered them, that kept her so amazingly young, as though that speck of the world in which they lived had become detached from the portion where the rest of us lived, continuing on its path to the land of shadows, where Grandma was already wandering. And so, what at first had merely been a postponement had ended up being a kind of immortality whose purpose she still couldn't fathom, but that united them in a way nothing else could, banishing them from time, exempting them from the painstaking disintegration all the rest of us were heading for.

Putting away the letter, I stared at the man behind the curtain, who gave a vague nod of the head that perhaps he wanted to seem evocative. Eva had constructed a lovely tale that was not only based on what he had told me the one time we had talked but it also beautifully justified the vigorous outline behind the drape that was so far removed from the tremors and sagging of old age. I was pleased I could return him a tale akin to his own, an elegant way to convey to him that I accepted his lies that had more beauty than logic. After all, the reasons why he was there were up to him.

I had imagined that the reading of Eva's letter would be the perfect goodbye, and so I stood up ready to recover my suitcases and leave. Instead, I took a step forward, grasped the curtain, and pulled it back with a simple, unceremonious gesture, wondering why I had never done so before and why I was doing it now. It had been fear that had kept Grandma from opening the curtain; Eva, because she intuited that the only thing keeping her from disappointment was precisely its mystery; and Marta, perhaps because she would not have been able to confront the gaze of the only witness to her misdemeanors. I, though, had no reason not to do so, although it wasn't curiosity that now compelled me, but the hope that the secret hidden by the curtain might somehow provide an excuse not to have to face my own destiny, a reason that might relieve me of the wearisome obligation of having to begin a new life with such a tired soul.

The man behind the curtain was an ordinary-looking individual of about forty years old, with skinny, bony shoulders, sharp features, and the face of an usher. I have no idea what I was hoping to discover behind the curtain, but I was disappointed to find someone so unremarkable, with no distinguishing feature about him that might merit him hiding in my living room—although I had no idea what that feature might be. He looked at me reluctantly, as though he regretted my action while at the same time approving it, or as if he could not condemn it because he himself had done the same in the past. We stood there staring at one another for a while, not knowing what to say. Then, after casting a nostalgic glance round the room and giving me a faint smile of farewell, he walked stiffly over to the door and renounced the apartment.

I was left on my own there for the first time, standing by the pulled-back curtain. I saw the strange emptiness that the absence of the man had left in the living room and couldn't resist taking his place to observe how he had seen our lives. It was a huge relief when I felt the wall at my back and my heels against the skirting board. I drew the curtain across, simply intending to faithfully reproduce all the details. But as I did so, I realized this was how Virtudes's husband had disappeared, and understood that he had been substituted in turn by the next tenant, so initiating a chain of disappearances that was now continuing with my own and threatened to perpetuate itself through the centuries, always with one man, a man in love who was waiting, heart aflame, for a woman—who by now was nothing more than a memory—to pull back the curtain.

The Heart and Other Viscera

On my birthday, Marcelo gave me his gallbladder. To celebrate, we had chosen one of those intimate restaurants where the waiters wander between the tables like ghosts, filling glasses or sweeping up crumbs with furtive gestures. At first glance, I didn't realize what that wrinkled, greenish chili pepper he was handing me in a jar was.

"It's my gallbladder," he explained, pointing to the place on his side where it had lodged like a bullet before it ended up in the jar. "I'm giving it you as a token that my love for you will always be free of bile," he said with cheerful grandiloquence. He sat staring at me very seriously, waiting for my reaction like someone who has just shown a photo of his children.

Love without bile. All right, got it. We had only been together for four months, but I was already beginning to discover that Marcelo was very fond of that kind of symbolism.

Maybe that was why he could not disguise his disappointment at the diamond-patterned necktie I gave him for his birthday two months later. His lack of enthusiasm made the loving process of choosing that particular pattern, which had taken up the whole of my morning, seem ridiculous. At the same time, I admit I was hopeful that he might take my gesture as a suggestion: a gift could also come from a shop window; it did not have to be the result of any dramatic bodily excision. Over the following months, I never saw him wear the tie, but his behavior led me to believe he had understood the message. Or so I thought until our first anniversary, when, with increasing horror, one by one I opened the five small boxes laid out on the table and discovered the ring finger, forefinger, thumb, and eventually all five fingers from his left hand, which only then crawled out of the lair of his pocket to demonstrate the painstaking pruning to which it had been submitted.

Marcelo had as little need of his fingers as he did of his gallbladder. He was a top executive in a multinational company and had a harem of secretaries at his disposal whom he could control merely by means of his voice. Like a stork, he had built his nest high in the clouds, at the top of a tower clad in glass and steel. If you peered at it from down below, you became as giddy as a pregnant woman, overwhelmed by a vertigo of insignificance from which it was difficult to recover. One rainy day, I had ventured inside for the first time with my résumé under my arm and a leaden vise gripping my heart, hoping to obtain one of the vacancies I had seen advertised in the newspaper. I didn't get the job, but I was lucky enough to bump into the monarch of this carpeted realm and to spill my coffee on his most expensive jacket. To Marcelo, accustomed as he was to pop-up women, females as curvaceous as they were sensual, my ethereal appearance and professor's spectacles must have seemed to him a very different proposition. He saw me as a heart where he could settle without fear of being bored, someone from whom he could extract a genuine moan, maybe one of those words defined in encyclopedias. In a daze that was a mix of enchantment and amusement, he allowed his jacket to be cleaned, while his business mind was busy considering a merger with this girl who never stopped apologizing desperately, although underneath it was not hard to glimpse her annoyance, as if deep down she thought the blame for their collision was all on his side.

He invited me to dinner the next evening and we fell in love before dessert, slightly embarrassed, as if falling in love was meant to be a slow surrender of the heart, a feeling that could only gush like a geyser in novels. Our love had a great deal of magic about it, like the inevitable attraction of a magnet and iron filings; a madness to which we had to surrender ourselves completely. I didn't know what Marcelo saw in me, but whatever it was seemed to me as magical as it was permanent. For my part, I wasn't seduced so much by the suave, gentle manners of someone who for years had not had to shout, as by the unforgettable look of helplessness in his eyes when he let his guard down, when all of a sudden he seemed to be struck by the disturbing certainty that he was nothing but a joke. He had gotten to where he was so easily, without having to stain his clothes with the sweat of effort, that his success seemed to him something anyone remotely intelligent could achieve. This made him terribly vulnerable within his invulnerability, a beggar dressed in prince's clothing. That insecurity, that twitch of humiliation and bewilderment that occasionally took hold of him, spoke of a fragile soul. It made him, despite his determined air and the swagger of an Adonis polished at the gym, a frail creature who was easy to love and as moving as a sparrow fallen from its nest.

I have to confess, though, that nothing about him could have forewarned me of his tendency to chop himself into bits. But after the little number with the fingers, I was ready for anything. I awaited our next celebration with great curiosity, although in the end his third gift did not come as any great surprise. I knew what it was even before I opened the box; in fact, from the moment he entered the restaurant with a patch over his left eye. After unwrapping our gifts, we peered at each other silently for a long while, studying each other with looks that spoke above all of resigned acceptance, of surrendering to the other's little whims: me toying with the glistening marble of his eye, and him with a pair of sunglasses that wouldn't be much use to him.

Young brides-to-be usually buy a chest to keep their dowry in. I had to make do with a freezer. And there, in its tundra belly, I stored the man I loved. Marcelo had more money than he could spend, and he could buy everything with it, including a team of unscrupulous surgeons willing to saw his body to pieces in the operating theater he had built in his basement. It was from there that Marcelo, or what was left of him, now worked, conveying by phone precise instructions for his tower to continue to soar upward. And all he needed for that was his tongue. No one in his firm could suspect that his absence was due to anything apart from his privileges as a boss, or because he was devoting himself exclusively to the lover they speculated he had. And no one, but no one, knew he was busy with those joyful, repeated mutilations, except the team of butchers who sliced him up without asking any questions, the two nurses looking after him, and the aforementioned lover.

In the meantime, the months were going by almost without my noticing, and I still couldn't find a job that lasted more than a week. There even came a moment when I stopped looking, because I suspected Marcelo was responsible for my sudden dismissals and that, in an excessive desire to protect me, he wanted to save me from any wear and tear. So I gave up trying to enter the world of work and instead dedicated myself to endless leisure. I took long walks in the park, went to the movies, did yoga, and even became a daytime television soap opera addict. The nights, though, I kept entirely for the guardian angel who had created this little girl's life for me. We had picnics by the fireside, giggling as we emptied several bottles of wine, until a more lustful glance than normal incited us to come together on the hearthrug. Then, feeling the gentle warmth of the flames on my back, I slowly kissed the absences, the gaps in his body, before giving myself to him slowly, like a gift he had the whole night to open. It could have been paradise but for the fact that I was unable to forget that I was embracing a man who was constantly fleeing, a man determined to dismantle himself.

After each celebration—and there were lots of them, because everything seemed to Marcelo worthy of being celebrated—I went home with another piece of his body. Over the next few months, I carefully wrapped in transparent plastic bags his kidneys, the strange slippers of his feet, the arms that embraced me, the hailstones of his teeth, the hand orphaned of its fingers. Some stormy nights, I imagined with awe that while Marcelo was stubbornly and diligently decimating himself in his basement, in the icy dungeon of my freezer a different Marcelo, a kind of lost, incomplete, and sinister twin brother who was as linked to him as a negative was taking shape, patiently reconstituting himself, just waiting for the moment when he became presentable enough to leap out and embrace me.

One fine day, as I was wrapping his latest gift, I realized with horror how routine all this had become for me. Almost without becoming aware of it, the passing of the months had effaced all remaining trace of surprise, so that now all I did was regard Marcelo's conscientious dismembering as inevitable. I even tried to find a reason for it. Marcelo was reducing himself, minimizing himself, stripping off everything superfluous in a harsh journey toward his most basic essence. But for what purpose? Within a few weeks, he had substituted his crutches for a motorized wheelchair, a sophisticated jalopy he went around everywhere in. Eventually, he decided to acquire one of those little guide monkeys. From the start, my relationship with the ape was one of mutual mistrust. I was horrified to see the monkey obey Marcelo's orders almost before he had given them; I couldn't bear to see the animal giving him a drink or combing his hair with maternal, solicitous haste. But the night that I watched incredulously as the primate mimicked by the insistent trombone movement of his little hand the only desire that Marcelo could feel by this stage of his dismemberment, I understood that all this had gone way too far.

I had to put a stop to this nonsense right away! And there was only one way to do that: if I was the accomplice in that demented slicing, all I had to do was to leave his side to put a stop to his imminent disintegration. But how could I abandon a man who had given me so much? The only way to do so was to approach it from a different angle, to interpret his exercise in dissection as an act of tremendous egotism, to consider that Marcelo was only offering me what he did not need, that the tender carving up of his body was exactly akin to giving the church the clothes you no longer wear. I confess that however hard I tried to view his dismemberment in this way, I did not succeed. Marcelo loved me. I only had to see how he was giving himself to me. All that was left was for him to give me his heart.

He gave it to me one rainy night, in a cooler filled with ice. Without my being aware of it, as if they had ganged up on me, several green men placed it in my chest to replace my own, which had chosen that night to reveal how weak it was. I knew nothing about the exchange until the next day, when I woke up in a hospital room with a huge scar between my breasts. I was surprised to find myself surrounded by a swarm of doctors and nurses who were celebrating my return from the shadows. They said I had slipped away and come to them, very ill prepared, the previous night. I immediately recalled the sudden tingling in my left arm just before dinner, and then the stabbing pain in my chest that left me in darkness. But everything had turned out fine, because they had immediately found a donor heart. From now on, I simply had to take care of myself, to lead as quiet a life as possible. I listened to the surgeons' explanations in a daze, as if they were talking about someone else, still trying to get my bearings.

Due to the effects of the anesthetic, the world came together for me only very tentatively, as if it was obeying the erratic dictates of some octogenarian demigod: the window beyond which a radiant morning was forming, the gaggle of doctors, the crucifix on the wall with its emaciated Christ, the visitors' chair in which Marcelo's lawyer was sitting. He was a friendly, well-groomed sort, so pink it always looked as if he had just emerged from a steaming-hot shower. When I was with Marcelo, I had been present at several of his discreet but decisive appearances. He appeared out of nowhere, perfectly naturally, wherever we might be, and after bestowing a polite smile on me, laid a couple of incisive phrases in Marcelo's ear, after which he nodded or shook his head forcefully, as if these movements were some kind of exorcism that would allow him to vanish once more into thin air. I have to admit he was the last person I expected to see in the hospital. And yet there he was, blending in with his surroundings, seated in the chair as impassively as a ventriloquist's dummy, simply waiting. And this time too his performance was a tribute to brevity. As soon as the doctors left the room, he stood up and handed me Marcelo's parting gift: a heart-shaped box. Then, after expressing his delight at the success of the transplant, he bowed and disappeared before I could even ask where his boss was.

But the answer lay inside the box; I only had to open it. Inside were two envelopes. One contained the electrocardiogram I had been given at Marcelo's firm the morning I had gone there applying for a job. In the other, I found a letter from him. I immediately recognized the spidery writing of someone learning to write with their mouth. On those sheets of paper, Marcelo responded definitively to all the questions I had never asked him. As I read his words, my hand shook and my eyes brimmed with tears. As logical as he was sentimental, Marcelo began by going back to the first morning we met. I was able to confirm that I caused the impact on him I had always suspected. He devoted a couple of paragraphs to praising my charms: my sprite-like appearance, my lucid gaze, the courage of someone who has had to fight for everything that he thought he could perceive in every one of my gestures. This was followed by a long list of attributes that were far from common in the rarefied atmosphere where he moved. Marcelo was fed up with gorgeous women incapable of arousing anything in him apart from biological yearnings. He had become immune to the showy, excessive, faultless beauty all around him. It was something that he already felt, but that until he met me had been only a vague sense of unease. That day, however, striving to understand why my sudden appearance had stirred him up so much, he suddenly realized how he detested the sophisticated lack of authenticity that prevailed in his realm. Prey to a strange impulse, he remained in his office until daylight was completely extinguished and the tower was empty. Abandoning his aerie, he spurned the elevators and walked down through the different floors, passing through each of the regions that made up his kingdom in a slow, nostalgic tour, like a ghost setting out on its rounds. He went through empty rooms and offices until he reached the recruitment department. There, his pulse racing with schoolboy excitement, he searched for my file among the piles strewn over the desks, desperate to know my name, age, and likes and dislikes, to discover everything about me before that first fateful meeting that had intertwined our destinies once and for all. It angered him to find the file among those who had been turned down, but his blood ran cold when he discovered that the reason for it was an incurable myocardial ischemia. According to his medical team, he had fallen in love with a woman who, unbeknownst to her, was afflicted with a damaged heart, a heart like a time bomb waiting to explode in the middle of her chest. Caressing the file, Marcelo thought things over for a long while. There was no solution to the illness but a transplant. And in his own chest he had a strong, healthy heart he did not know what to do with. Taking out his lighter, he brought the flame to the tip of the folder and watched it burn with a complicit smile. The next day, no woman was going to receive the news that she was condemned to die. That night, sitting in the darkness in the midst of mountains of files, Marcelo took stock, weighed everything up, and finally decided to redeem his worthless existence with a magnanimous act. He would look after this stranger, build a world without anxiety for her, fulfill her every desire, like a Pygmalion from the heights. And finally, when the moment came, he would make the sacrifice that would save both that woman's life and his own.

The very next morning, he set to work. He phoned me at home to inform me that I did not fit the profile they were looking for, and to invite me to have the coffee I had spilled. The fact that I might also fall in love with him was not absolutely necessary, but it made everything easier. Every night, Marcelo watched me smile, stroke his hand, and celebrate his witty remarks, and he smiled as well, because he had confirmed that his heart and my body would not reject each other, since he knew that in each and every one of the hospitals in the city a team of surgeons was waiting like musketeers on guard, because the entire universe was on high alert. The idea of chopping himself up only occurred to him later on. And he didn't do this so that when the moment of truth came for him to donate his heart nothing would make him back out. He embarked on his meticulous subtractions moved by the desire to see the effect his loving donations had on me, as he would not be there to see the expression on my face when he gave me his final gift. He was hoping that at the very least I would not hate him.

My tears soaked the last page of his letter. Moved so much I was unable to stop weeping, I raised my hand to my heart. Beneath my fingertips, I felt Marcelo's heartbeats; heartbeats that often, as I slept curled up on his chest, I had heard like a calm, protective, subterranean rumble—a rhythm breathing life into the man who in turn gave me life. Now those heartbeats belonged to me. They were mine. If we disregard the contents of the freezer, they were all I had left of Marcelo.

I had a lengthy convalescence in which to absorb the enormity of his gesture. On leaving the hospital, I discovered that Marcelo had given me not only his heart, but also his house and enough money to enable me to live the quiet life the doctors were recommending. I devoted myself to it. I went back to my yoga classes and walks in the park, but I exchanged soap operas for jigsaw puzzles. And despite the fact that some nights his absence seemed to me unbearable, and all I wanted to do was to surrender, give in, to put an end to this borrowed existence that seemed to me like a jail sentence, I never did.

I had to understand that, despite being on my own, I really wasn't. Marcelo ran through my veins, saw through my eyes, beat inside my chest. All I had to do was lead a life worthy of his sacrifice. To live for us both. Until the day that he took pity and decided to end the heartbeats.

The Seven (or So) Lives of Sebastian Mingorance

The weatherman had warned of it two days in advance: a storm was coming that weekend. He delivered this forecast with total self-assurance, framed by an image of the country as seen by the celestial eye of the weather satellite, the area of low pressure resembling the entrails of a burst pillow. And for once, he appeared to be right, thought Sebastian Mingorance, studying the gray, unforgiving sky from his bedroom window, through which glided enormous black clouds, sinister as stealth bombers. This collusion of clouds frustrated his plans to go fishing, forcing him to spend the weekend confined to his tiny bachelor pad. And long may it remain so, he would declare to his friends when they met for a drink at the bar, although it was just a pretense, to show he was happy with what he had to that censorial group of first-time fathers, callow youths with dark circles under their eyes, whose continuity had been achieved with a pelvic thrust; pitiful cabin boys awash in a sea of bottles and diapers. And so Sebastian Mingorance resigned himself to a tedious day at home, fending off the claustrophobia of boredom by mainlining the drowsy opiate of television, or by playing solitaire, it made no difference; anything was better than succumbing to the humiliation of opening his briefcase and catching up on his reports. Anything. He made himself a cup of coffee and hurriedly pulled on some clothes to go out and buy the distraction of a newspaper before the storm broke.

When he reached the street, still in the doorway after sprinting downstairs, he was overwhelmed by his customary paralysis. At the end of the street on the right was Felipe's newsstand. On the left was Bernardo's newsstand. The door to Mingorance's apartment block was exactly midway between the two. Felipe was a nervy youngster with a forward manner, who hawked his newspapers with exaggerated urgency as if performing a rescue operation. Bernardo, on the other hand, was a reserved old man with faltering gestures, who hawked his newspapers with discreet indifference, as if engaged in a contraband operation. Mingorance found both attitudes equally irritating, and as a result, he always had difficulty deciding which way to go; especially when, as now, he didn't have the right money, and would inevitably be given change: from Felipe, a tiresome handful of coins that would always escape as they were thrust into his palm, or, from Bernard, a sweaty assortment of coppers that would invariably miss the target of his upturned hand. Either way, Mingorance would find himself scrabbling on the ground for coins. Whether when he did so he received on the back of his head a blast of cheap tobacco or a whiff of hair of the dog was up to him. His final decision, taken without resorting to reason, which given the circumstances was completely pointless, never ceased to bemuse Mingorance. He never knew what made him turn right instead of left, or vice versa, although he sensed that the choice wasn't quite a conscious one. And since he considered it excessively demeaning to give the credit to his feet, he preferred to imagine it had nothing to do with him, and that instead a higher power, a kind of cosmic puppet master, was guiding him in one direction or the other, following some mysterious design.

On that Saturday, then, for no particular reason, Mingorance turned left when he could just have easily turned right. Conversely, Mingorance I the Irresolute, whom we shall designate thus to distinguish him from the original for reasons that will soon become clear, turned right when he could just as easily have turned left. At the end of the street, cocooned in the bunker of his newsstand, his newspapers protected beneath plastic sheeting, Bernardo watched the advancing storm clouds with a knowing eye, as Noah must have studied the sky moments before the prophesied flood. At the far end of the street, Fernando contemplated the rain clouds with an apathy that revealed his generation's inbred foolish anti-conformism, leaving it until the last moment to cover his newspapers. The first raindrops surprised Mingorance and

Mingorance I the Irresolute as they were picking up the coins strewn on the ground. Both shielded their heads with their newspapers, and made for the doorway to their building, trotting in that silly way that isn't quite running, but that, when performed elegantly, is a supple movement of the legs that can amount to a brief and somewhat striking display of physical prowess. During his little sprint, Mingorance I the Irresolute narrowly avoided colliding with his neighbor from across the street, also on his way to the newsstand, although his trot was a great deal more lithe and synchronized, suggesting calf muscles honed on an exercise bike. Mingorance I the Irresolute eyed him with contempt. He only knew his neighbor by sight, from spying on him out of his window, and yet he felt the same hatred for him as he would if he had confessed during a drunken spree that he liked to rub himself against nine-year-old girls on public transport. In fact, he represented everything that Mingorance I the Irresolute secretly longed to be: with his denim jeans and shoulder-length hair, he looked like a cool teenager, one of those people with the cosmopolitan air of an adventurer, who always applies the tourniquets when there's a train crash.

He was brooding over this when he spotted the girl on the sidewalk, the rain making her red curls bedraggled. Her slender body was leaning over a bicycle chained to an orange tree, her pearl-white hand stubbornly squeezing the back tire as if she refused to accept that she lived in such a sickeningly cinematic world, where punctures always happen during a downpour. Their gazes collided conveniently and, even as Mingorance I the Irresolute's step slowed, by way of compensation his pulse quickened. All that beauty concentrated in one woman, right there, in the middle of nowhere, within anyone's grasp, took his breath clean away. It was obvious she wasn't local but rather was there on an errand or a social visit, and that with her bicycle out of service she would have trouble getting home. Seeing her stranded as the rain poured more heavily, desperately searching the buildings with no sheltering doorways and the spindly orange trees even as the rising wind tore at her coat, led Mingorance I the Irresolute to consider the possibility of helping her out. He seriously thought of going up to her and inviting her for a coffee in his apartment until the storm blew over, but was dissuaded by the certainty that he would be unable to accompany the offer with a smile free from insinuation and awkwardness. He had been chaste for many years, and the mere idea of her following him into his lair filled his veins with a clumsy, feverish desire. He doubted he would even make it to the front door, and imagined pouncing on her in the hallway, grunting as he took her on the landing. Or, what was worse, he imagined reaching the apartment safe and sound, his fingers abashed by her celestial curves, his manhood dead and buried before all that beauty. In short, he imagined himself reduced to a shy, ungainly teenager, who, with tragic symbolism, would end up spilling his coffee all over her skirt. Clearly, the budget for the film of his life didn't stretch to include a woman like her. And so, true to his name, Mingorance I the Irresolute walked on by, cravenly leaving her to the rigors of the weather, excusing his lack of courage with a foolish grin, even as he puzzled over the way others always get the best things in life, already thinking about arriving home and abandoning himself to another of those sad, bitter masturbation sessions that punctuated his bachelorhood.

However, Mingorance II the Intrepid had other plans. Compelled possibly by the many years of famine, by a frustration that threatened to become chronic, and because the memory of Belen's docile blow jobs had all but faded—Belen, that incompetent, bucktoothed secretary, whose brief sojourn at the company was justified only by her ability to alleviate the tensions of practically the entire male staff with her rabbit-like mouth. For this and possibly a thousand other reasons too tedious and numerous to mention, Mingorance II the Intrepid told himself that in the end we construct our own lives, brick by brick, and if we keep missing the opportunities, we will have difficulty getting anywhere. And so, taking advantage of the timely cloudburst backed up by distant rumbles of thunder, Mingorance II the Intrepid approached with his most innocent smile that rare, exotic butterfly suddenly within reach of his net.

Halting at a prudent distance, he debated whether or not to take another step forward, the way tigers do when confronted by a rustle in the undergrowth, and then, in a reedy voice, dizzy from the scent of perfume and female perspiration reaching him on the breeze, he invited her up to his place for coffee. She looked at him with a mixture of appreciation and mistrust, as though speculating about the possible dangers of being locked in an apartment with a stranger in this era of extravagant perversions. However, the timid fellow holding his paper over his head must have struck her as harmless, friendly even, because, after scrutinizing the sky filling with leaden clouds, she accepted the offer with a polite smile. Although taken aback by her acceptance of his offer, Mingorance II the Intrepid managed gallantly to hoist the bicycle onto his shoulder and set off toward his lair, grateful for the rain that hid his tears as the pedal dug painfully into his shoulder blade. The wind flung the dead leaves against the passersby like ninja stars. Suddenly plunged into the silence of a lengthy courtship, they reached the doorway to his building, passing on the way Mingorance I the Irresolute, who was watching the neighbor opposite as he chatted excitedly to the girl with the bicycle. He looked on with infinite sadness as she examined the storm clouds then nodded with a smile, while his neighbor hoisted her bicycle onto his shoulder, taking care not to let the pedal dig in to him. They crossed the road struggling against the wind: he disgustingly solid, like a menhir; she touchingly fragile, like a hut made of straw. Giggling like a couple of kids, they reached the entrance, while Mingorance I the Irresolute, the girl's laughter piercing his heart like a glass shard, began to mount the stairs, treading close on the heels of Mingorance II the Intrepid, who was carrying a bicycle and a dream.

Mingorance didn't even hear them enter, distracted as he was at his window. He was watching the arrival of the storm with a melancholy that was doubly melancholic, for, added to the sadness one always feels on rainy days, there was the sight of his neighbor opposite, festooned with a punctured bicycle, approaching the entrance to his building accompanied by a young girl with a shock of red hair. Yet again, his neighbor seemed determined to show him that he knew how to live life, that he was able to get the best out of it even in the most adverse circumstances, including a redhead in the midst of a storm. Mingorance spied on him with contempt. He only knew him by sight, and yet he felt the same hatred for him as he would if he had confessed during a drunken spree to knowing someone in the morgue who let him do things to dead people. He represented everything Mingorance secretly longed to be: he was one of those people who, when a ship is sinking and the passengers are crammed onto the lifeboats, appears at the last moment clutching a little girl's lost dog, as if he had pulled it out of a hat.

Such was life, thought Mingorance; some people feast on everything, while others content themselves with the crumbs. And he had always found a kind of bitter irony in the fact that their buildings were almost identical, so much so that they were like reflections, and that they happened to live in the same apartment on the same floor, as if fate had arranged things that way on purpose, to make them goad each other on, to make one feel like the negative of the other. He sat down in the armchair and smoothed out the crumpled newspaper, still going over in his mind the scene he had just witnessed. Why did he never bump into beautiful redheads in the rain? Why did his life seem so impervious to such pleasurable coincidences, to chance encounters with the promise of romance? Why did his life always run along such sterile, orderly tracks? What if he had decided to walk toward the right, toward Felipe's newsstand, and had come across her, stranded in the rain, pleading for shelter with her eyes? But who was he trying to kid? If that had happened, he would be equally alone now in his apartment, annoyed at the innate shyness that would have prevented him from helping her. Or so he concluded, spreading the newspaper on his knees, which were at right angles to those of Mingorance I the Irresolute, who was sitting in the armchair beside him, lamenting the innate shyness that had prevented him from helping the redhead—whom, only a few feet away, Mingorance II the Intrepid was busy relieving of her coat with reverential fingers.

As if the act of hanging the dripping wet coat on the hook were a kind of cue, Mingorance I the Irresolute leaped from his chair and hurried over to the window. He would suffer, he knew, but he couldn't tear himself away from the scene that should have been his: through the window, he watched his neighbor divest the woman of her dripping coat, offer her a seat, hand her a towel. And all those apparently harmless gestures, which were the same ones Mingorance II the Intrepid was carrying out behind him, seemed in his rival to be links in an implacable chain repeated endlessly, a strategic deployment of pieces with the sole aim of pouncing on her. He moved away from the window when his neighbor appeared with the coffee. He had already seen what would come next a thousand times on television: the coffee spilled on her blouse as if by accident, his handkerchief at the ready to fix the problem. Cursing his luck, he sat down next to the young girl drying her red hair with his towel as she shouted, "Three sugars," in the direction of the kitchen. Mingorance II the Intrepid silently cursed his lack of forethought as he contemplated the dregs in the sugar bowl. He scraped it together carefully, just about filling the third teaspoon with that brown sugar that always sticks to the sides, a gesture that made him feel shamefully stingy and reaffirmed his desire to be a different person, better than any uplifting example from the Bible. Everyday reality demonstrated that Mingorance II the Intrepid was a terribly practical person, one of those men who only fill the sugar bowl when its depletion has become a reality rather than an illusion. Similarly, for example, on the rare occasions when he went out partying with his friends, he never carried an extraneous object in his wallet. Taking a condom with him seemed to him like something a Boy Scout would do, a supremely pretentious gesture, and no woman had ever managed to persuade him otherwise. And yet, faced with the unhappy incident of the sugar, he had to admit that he would get nowhere with this kind of behavior, much less be the equal of his ineffable neighbor, whose drawers were probably brimming with prophylactics and spermicides, and who doubtless stored sachets of sugar in jars, beneath the carpet or taped under his armpits, because you never knew when an emergency might crop up.

While a tormented Mingorance I the Irresolute imagined returning from the kitchen with two piping-hot cups of coffee on a stylish-looking tray to show the woman that he was a sophisticated sort who kept up with the latest trends, Mingorance II the Intrepid returned to the living room with two Duralex cups on a moldy tray he had dug out of the bottom of the cupboard, and Mingorance scanned the newspaper for a crime of passion to brighten up his morning. He was looking for tragedies in the lives of others that made his own seem better in comparison, or that would at least keep him entertained: a nurse commanded by God to poison her patients; a domestic argument resolved with a hammer blow; a dog that had trailed its master all the way to the Andes—anything would do. But the newspaper was dull, proving that the previous day had been an interval of sorts, a kind of religious holiday for rapists and murderers. Oblivious to his lust for tragedies, the redhead picked up her coffee, cheeks flushing as she took a long, deep, one might say fervent, sip accompanied by a darkly intimate sigh of satisfaction. Mingorance II the Intrepid picked up his cup, also attempting to evoke coffee's legendary ability to create closeness—something he knew about from advertisements rather than from personal experience. However, he failed miserably, swilling the coffee around in his mouth for too long as if he were gargling, and then ending with a yelp of hemorrhoid pain more intimate than he had intended. The fortuitous, suggestive return of their two cups to the tray sparked off a conversation that began meanderingly with the usual faltering questions and hurried, clichéd replies, confused comments that were abandoned in midstream for being overly intricate, but that, to Mingorance II the Intrepid's astonishment, soon began to flow easily and even pleasantly. For once, talking to a woman seemed to him relaxing and enjoyable, and he soon discovered that she possessed a ready laugh, which bubbled over at the slightest witticism on his part, a natural laugh that both surprised and reassured him. It inspired in him a flowery lyricism and a flamboyant piquancy, brought out a subtle, inventive humor he didn't know he possessed. Amid laughter and sips of coffee, with the patter of rain creating an even cozier atmosphere in the living room, they decoded each other to the point of discovering that they were completely opposite, not to say opposed. Her name was Claudia. She had studied piano and had traveled all over the world as a member of a philharmonic orchestra, leading a nomadic, rewarding life filled with dramatic events, a life she had recently renounced so as to ground herself, exhausted and with a lot of emotional scars that had left her cynical and cautious. For his part, he remembered having once gone on a school trip to Granada, and now he worked in an office nearby. He liked to take a stroll in the evenings, but was careful never to stray from his neighborhood. He ate dinner at the Chinese restaurant on the corner and went fishing on the weekends, to distinguish them from workdays. He admitted all this without realizing it, too immersed in the conversation to think of making up lies, to create an imaginary existence that didn't seem so pitiful, but what was done was done, and she was observing him with entomological curiosity, possibly wondering where the catch was, or—Mingorance II the Intrepid dared to hope in a sudden flash of optimism—imagining what it would be like to be loved by a man like him, capable of revealing himself with a candor so brutal it verged on the obscene; someone straightforward and without a mask, with a heart seemingly new to love. And, while they were on the subject, he might have added that she only need ask and he would love her with a devotion that would erase the bleakness of all those disastrous nocturnal liaisons in foreign lands that haunted her gaze. But he didn't have the courage for that. Instead, he let himself be examined by Claudia's expert eye, which appraised him with, he thought, a certain eagerness, as she might a rare, exotic butterfly that was suddenly within reach of her net.

Oblivious to his thirst for happiness, Mingorance I the Irresolute debated whether to spend his Saturday sprawled on the sofa, or to cross the street to his neighbor's apartment and reclaim what was his, before the neighbor laid his grubby paws on her. He imagined himself pounding frantically on the door, interrupting the idyllic scene taking place inside with a rambling, cliché-ridden speech about missed opportunities— an approach that, according to the teachings of the television, women found romantically irresistible as well as profitable. In the end, though, he rejected the idea, which on consideration seemed too foolish.

However, Mingorance III the Brave leaped to his feet and ran downstairs. At heart, he was a lover of lost causes. He paused for a few moments in the street, watching with disgust the amorous advances of his neighbor, his supple, feline precision as he stalked his quarry, ready to pounce. After nearly half an hour watching in the rain, the courage Mingorance III the Brave needed finally flared up inside him, mighty and invincible, on par with the flu virus that was taking hold, though far less conspicuously. He ran up the stairs and pounded on the door with calculated frenzy. No sooner had it swung open than he launched into his speech aimed at softening the young woman's heart. She gazed at him in shock, too astonished to hear what he was saying, which at best was rather garbled. Mingorance III the Brave realized then, with the inestimable help of the full-length mirror in the hallway, that some romantic gestures can appear ridiculous if not performed with sufficient conviction. He was incensed when his neighbor started to nod and clap him on the shoulder, like someone trying to pacify a dangerous lunatic. Before he knew it, he found himself being propelled toward the stairs by an apparently friendly pair of hands, which nevertheless displayed a profound knowledge of martial arts each time he tried to turn around. These kindly claws forced him to make a last effort to shake himself free. The unexpected gesture took his neighbor by complete surprise.

He teetered on the edge of the stairwell for a few nail-biting seconds before plunging downward. Mingorance III the Brave watched him bounce off the steps with what seemed to him excessive flamboyance, until he reached the landing below, where he came to a lifeless halt, his neck and limbs forming the oddest of angles, as if to show off their double-jointedness. The monstrosity of the situation paralyzed Mingorance III the Brave. But not the girl, who assimilated what had happened before he did, and even managed to interpret it in her own way, as she fled, terrified, down the stairs. Uncertain whether or not he should try to stop her, Mingorance III the Brave watched her step over the body in disgust, a reaction he found pleasing despite the horrific circumstances, before continuing her flight. When the clatter of her shoes had dwindled in the distance, all he could hear was the rain beating down and giving the city a blurred, ghostly appearance.

Meanwhile, Mingorance had decided to have lunch at the Chinese restaurant. Unaware that part of him had killed a man, he leaped clumsily over the puddles in his yellow raincoat, like something from an incongruous parody of a bucolic scene, until he found himself standing outside the restaurant. He placed his hand on the red double doors, flanked by a pair of elaborate ornamental dragons, and paused before disturbing the shrine-like silence that exists inside Asian eateries. In fact, he realized suddenly, he was in no mood to enter the artificial universe awaiting him on the far side of the door, or to surrender with infinite patience to consuming one of those seemingly endless dishes of chopped food. But, more than that, he was in no mood to do so under the scrutiny of the elderly Chinaman who never took his eyes off him as he sat in the lotus position on his patriarchal cushion. If the waitresses treated him with perfunctory indifference, the old man fixed him with a cold stare that seemed to Mingorance brimming with dark, ancestral condemnation. It was obvious that he considered Mingorance's life idle and profane, utterly at odds with everything that surrounded him, and wholly dishonorable. And the truth was that, after being irradiated by those eyes for a while, Mingorance would briefly examine his own conscience and end up agreeing with the old man, and would invariably creep out of the restaurant like the lowliest of worms. And so now he turned on his heel and retraced his steps. Pausing before the entrance to his apartment block, he contemplated walking to the garage, climbing into his car, and driving aimlessly around the outskirts of the city, on a whim, simply to experience a world that beneath that heavy rainfall must seem as intimate as it did deserted. In the end, he rejected the idea as foolish. As he mounted the stairs, he made an astonishing list of the number of times in a day we have to make a decision, however trivial and insignificant it might be. And he wondered what consequences each decision entailed, whether the life we live in the end is better than the ones we reject.

And as Mingorance IV the Abducted set off toward the garage, whistling as he went, Mingorance V the Untimely, who was in no mood for philosophizing and could have eaten a horse, resolutely pushed open the door to the restaurant. He contemplated the interior, resigned and dripping wet: the elaborate murals, the discreet Muzak, the empty tables due to the rain, and at the far end, as he had feared, the old Chinaman sitting calmly on his cushion. Except that today, unlike other days, leveled at his head was a gun, which a trembling hand was struggling to keep steady. It took Mingorance V the Untimely several seconds to realize that he had arrived in the midst of a holdup. The aggressor, a typical drug addict, was the only one who hadn't noticed him walk in, as he was too busy threatening the old man and the waitresses and trying not to drop the gun. The three victims observed him solemnly over their assailant's shoulder, concealing their delight at the arrival of this unexpected savior in such an advantageous position. Mingorance V the Untimely realized that he couldn't exit the way he had come silently, as had been his intention. No, that was impossible. Presented with a situation that required a gallant gesture, he had no choice but to act the hero if he wanted to look himself in the face again, or continue to patronize the restaurant. The odds were in his favor, he concluded with a sigh. Even the arrangement of the tables offered a tempting, unobstructed pathway to the attacker, allowing a good run-up should he decide to charge rather than sneak up behind the man. And so Mingorance V the Untimely, noticing the old Chinaman's expectant eyes upon him and realizing he hadn't the necessary audacity for a catlike approach, launched into a mad dash toward the felon, who scarcely managed to turn around before being knocked to the ground by this fellow who had appeared out of nowhere. They rolled about on the floor, entwined like a pair of impassioned lovers. When the world stopped spinning, Mingorance V the Untimely found himself in the arms of a scrawny, malodorous body, which he wasn't quite sure what to do with. Such was his feeling of unreality that he only attempted to wrangle the gun from the man when he tried to point it at him. They struggled awkwardly, with none of the spectacularism of motion pictures, more like a couple of kids fighting over a toy: constipated grunts and a tangle of fingers around the cold, slippery metal object.

Mingorance V the Untimely gritted his teeth to contain a howl of frustration: the frenzy overwhelming him was due more to his fear of not giving a convincing enough performance in his role as defender than the prospect of being shot, which in his delirium he hadn't even considered. Suddenly, a series of sharp kicks rained down upon his adversary's face, and Mingorance V the Untimely realized that the waitresses had finally decided to intervene. He found himself holding the gun and, gasping, saw the shambling figure of his adversary as he fled the restaurant. He rose laboriously to his feet, wondering if the man would remember his face and devote the rest of his life to leaving dead cats outside his front door and systematically raping all his progeny regardless of their gender, and he feared for his mother, languishing in an old people's home with easy access, oblivious to the enemies her son was making in his life of violence. Then he had the impression of being plunged into a basket of freshly laundered towels: the waitresses had begun covering his face in a flutter of friendly caresses; one of them expressed concern over his split lip in staccato Spanish, possibly the same idiot who had aimed a kick at him in the heat of the moment, because he was nearest to her. Before he had a chance to react, Mingorance V the Untimely found himself seated at a table where, with a rapidity that defied the norm, plates of sweet and sour salad began to arrive, followed by fried rice, chicken with oysters, pork curry, and a thousand other courses, which were served up relentlessly, and which, to the delight of the appreciative employees, he did his best to demolish, grinning at them, with one swollen cheek, where someone had placed a dab of ointment. But the climax of all this madness came from the old patriarch, when Mingorance V the Untimely was wincing as he downed the small glass of liqueur he had been offered. To his astonishment, the old man rose from his cushion, and approached the table with spiderlike movements, stepping out of his purely decorative function. Looking straight at him with a determination that gave Mingorance V the Untimely the feeling of a hook picking the lock of his soul, the old man uttered a few muffled whispers and put a large ebony box down on the table. From it he extracted a *katana*, the blade of which was inscribed with a few characters. He bowed and placed the sword in the hands of Mingorance V the Untimely, who accepted the gift with a novice samurai's smile, even as he wondered whether from then on he would open the door of his apartment each morning only to find the old man keeping watch on the landing next to the milk.

Distracted at the window, Mingorance III the Brave didn't notice him cross the street on his way back to the apartment, brandishing the *katana* in the air. He was waiting with a kind of morbid anticipation for the police to arrive, not knowing whether the girl had reported him or not. But mostly he was trying to rid himself of the impression of death, which was clinging to his hands after he had been forced to carry his neighbor's corpse back to his apartment, where he had installed him on a chair. He could think of no way to atone for the man's death other than to remove him from the stairway. The gesture had been a rash one, a kind of posthumous affectionate gesture, and now that he was calmer, he had begun to fret over the fingerprints he must carelessly have left all over the apartment. But why was that worrying him now? He struggled to decide whether it had been a cold-blooded murder or a tragic accident, and wondered whether, if he decided the latter, he shouldn't remove all signs of his presence there, rather than cleaning up the crime scene. Yes, perhaps he should do his best to make the accident look like an accident. Then he started to sneeze, and was overcome by a general feeling of lethargy, which in turn made him even more indifferent toward the possible outcome of his involuntary crime.

Sitting on the sofa behind him, Mingorance was channel-hopping to dull his hunger, because, having ruled out the

Chinese restaurant, he had decided to skip lunch—after all, who knew what horrors might be lurking in the refrigerator of a bachelor who was in the habit of eating out? However, Mingorance I the Irresolute, compelled by a spirit of self-destruction, which he had been cultivating for years and had finally decided to bring to fruition on that stormy Saturday, was spreading out on the kitchen table the scraps of food from his fridge, all of which were well past their sell-by date and in an advanced stage of putrefaction. After reflecting at length, he reached the conclusion that the life we lead depends entirely on us, that we create or destroy it with the decisions we make, and that if, as had been proven beyond doubt, he was incapable of steering his existence toward happiness, he could at least send it careening into the abyss. He needed to find out whether he could take control of his own life or was merely a puppet, callously manipulated by someone else. More than anything, he needed to see death up close, smell its fetid breath. The only way to give his life meaning, he thought, was to risk losing it: the so-called compensatory power of loss. And so, he began to devour determinedly and even pleasurably his macabre picnic of rancid yogurt, moldy pâté, half-decaying oranges, and rotten sardines, as well as a large number of as-yet-unidentified varieties of mushroom. And if that didn't send him to his grave, it would at least cause him to view each day as a clean sheet where anything could happen, from losing his heart to a stranger amid cloudbursts and coffee, to being caught in a holdup, the only limitation being his imagination.

After hanging up his raincoat next to the redhead's overcoat so that the two dripping side by side created a puddle, which, if this were a romantic novel rather than an exercise in hypothetical procreation, would have formed a heart shape, Mingorance V the Untimely sat down on the sofa, contemplating with satisfaction his *katana*, while Mingorance turned his attention to a documentary about the animal world. This particular one was about the life and miracles of a merry band of leopards. At that precise moment, one of them was on the prowl, and the camera showed him, menacing and beautiful amid the undergrowth, stalking with a princely gait a gazelle that had strayed from the herd. Encouraged by Claudia's infectious laughter, although lacking any feline instinct, Mingorance II the Intrepid also began his pursuit. Quick and precise, the leopard prepared to pounce on his quarry, following to the letter the inexorable law of the savannah, and yet scarcely had he time to extend his claws, when, in an abrupt reversal of roles, the gazelle leaped on him, throwing him back onto the sofa, seeking out his neck, and tearing off his shirt buttons. When the world stopped spinning, Mingorance II the Intrepid found himself in the arms of a slender, fragrant body, which he wasn't quite sure what to do with. He only succeeded in making a single wish: that the providential storm would never end. He also prayed that God, who could to some extent be blamed for creating a world by piling up perishable items, might attempt to redeem himself by conceiving something that endured, and that when he did so, they would be the lucky ones. Thunderclaps scored the skies angrily, and Claudia's tongue scoured furiously inside his mouth. Her teeth bit into his lips, tugging at them. Mingorance II the Intrepid was forced to snatch her kisses like someone plucking berries from a bramble bush. Claudia had brought back from her European nights wild gestures, voluptuous wails, and frenzied spasms, to which Mingorance II the Intrepid was only able to respond with slow, lingering caresses, kisses in the most unlikely places, gestures designed to prolong the fleeting natures of pleasure. Baffled yet touched by this change of rhythm, she accepted this homely, earnest way of making love that left no scars, while on the television screen, and in his neighbor's window, the big cat created flowers of blood.

At last the storm abated, and sunlight struck the windows like a volley of stones. Seeping into the room, it shone on the pale, feverish face of Mingorance III the Brave; danced along the fine blade of Mingorance V the Untimely's *katana*; bathed the head of Mingorance in a saffron light as he dozed on the sofa; illuminated the death throes of Mingorance I the Irresolute as he lay writhing on the kitchen floor, sniffing the stench of death; and finally blessed the foolish grin on the lips of Mingorance II the Intrepid, curled up beneath a blanket with Claudia, their naked bodies fusing even as he let her caress the imprint of the pedal on his shoulder, daydreaming that it was the result of a duel of honor, feeling elated, hopeful, immortal even, with a new confidence in life, when what should he do but prove just how fragile happiness can be by delivering the hammer blow of an inopportune question, to which her reply, "Yes, three sugars, please," flooded his mind with the terrifying image of the empty sugar bowl. Cursing himself for not keeping his mouth shut, he abandoned her, got dressed, and went out onto the landing, where he confronted the jungle in which, for a brief moment, he had forgotten he lived, and into which he was now forced, damn it, to venture in search of sugar.

Once again, his path forked. In the upstairs apartment lived three widowed sisters who ran a small macramé business, who always became rather agitated whenever he called, as if he were a persistent suitor. Downstairs, surrounded by mounds of papers and blackboards, lived a reclusive physicist who would receive him in his dressing gown with several days' stubble on his chin and an unfriendly cat at his feet. Both alternatives were equally repugnant to Mingorance II the Intrepid, but as he didn't want to take root on the landing, he directed his steps toward the widows.

To step over the threshold of their apartment was to venture in to a three-way world, to experience the vertigo of three lives ruled by the number three. Three years separated the three sisters, although at a glance Mingorance II the Intrepid found it impossible to range them according to age, let alone remember their names, or spot any difference between the trio of wilted blossoms. As though in deference to some three-headed deity, they had married three brothers, who made up the wind section of a wedding orchestra, in a triple ceremony, and had lost their husbands in a three-car pileup on the National Route 3 one ill-fated third of March thirty-three years earlier. Mingorance II the Intrepid had pieced together this tragic trigonometry of their lives during his visits to borrow sugar or salt, and now, outside on the landing, he prepared himself for any fresh dizzying triplications he might have to add to the combination. As always, the macramé makers' door stood ajar, and while he understood that this was due to the difficulty of abandoning their task, which required all three of them, Mingorance II the Intrepid couldn't help considering it an obscene invitation, a veiled eagerness to be assaulted by anyone, a perpetual incitement to burglary, but above all to larceny, to the dishonoring of their already tainted honor.

He stepped gingerly into the dimly lit apartment reeking of boiled cauliflower. From the ceiling hung sinister, marsupial-shaped objects, revealed by flashes of lightning to be flowerpots, each in its respective macramé basket. At the far end of the apartment, the three widows were absorbed in their labors. Dark and focused, they gave the slightly repulsive impression of busy spiders. One sister was holding the ball from which the strings sprouted; another, opposite her, held the guiding thread; and a third plaited the knots. For a while, Mingorance II the Intrepid stood contemplating the rhythmic movement of those skeletal hands that unerringly decided where the threads should go in a mechanical, unconscious way. What most fascinated him were the lines the threads traced in the air, their strange, solitary meanderings before they rejoined the mother strand to be where they were subsumed into a fresh knot. From this tangle emerged a beautiful braid, whose splendor resided in the succession of knots, each no more than the remembrance of an aborted line that no longer existed, except perhaps as an echo traced briefly by the thread as it veered from its course, a pitiful voice of dissent against the designs of a snow-white hand that always chose the final pattern. That coil enclosed a thousand sacrificed dreams; it was made of suppositions, footprints in the sand. Seeing Mingorance II the Intrepid, the three sisters interrupted their task and rushed over to him, clucking like broody hens, fighting to peck his cheeks. It was as if he had been plunged into a basket of dirty linen. As soon as he had been given the sugar, he fled the apartment as fast as he could, as if escaping with the Holy Grail. He didn't even notice that one of the little packets had a tear in it, and that a sugary trail down the stairs betrayed his flight.

The physicist's apartment was in chaos. The walls were lined with blackboards, the tables stacked high with papers; saucers of milk lay dotted about the floor. Mingorance VI the Perplexed waited in what he assumed was the living room for his neighbor to return with the sugar, taking great care not to step on any of the saucers for fear that Schrödinger, the physicist's cat, might pounce on him from where he sat lying in wait. The physicist returned from the kitchen with his dressing gown in disarray and his hair even more disheveled, as if he'd had to hack a path through the undergrowth to reach the small packets of sugar he was holding, and Mingorance VI the Perplexed felt obliged to offer him a moment's conversation in return for his trouble. Contemplating the blackboard scrawled with equations in front of him, he was tempted to ask what problem he was attempting to solve. However, as he didn't consider himself equipped to be the custodian of any mystery from the numerical hereafter, he opted for something simpler, and inquired about the cat's name. Seemingly touched by his interest, the physicist smiled, and Mingorance VI the Perplexed realized he was about to be treated to a lengthy explanation. Launching into a speech that made Mingorance VI the Perplexed suspect that prior to retreating into his lair his neighbor had taught at some college or other, the physicist explained that Schrödinger was the name of a man who had locked his cat in a box with a device containing poison. The poison was released when an atom disintegrated, he continued, his voice growing sad, an atom that had exactly a 50 percent chance of disintegrating in a specific length of time. Schrödinger sealed the box and waited. His question was whether after the prescribed time had passed, the cat would be alive or dead. Mingorance VI the Perplexed shrugged, somewhat alarmed by the increasingly sinister gesticulations with which the physicist was illustrating his story. According to quantum theory, he went on, there was a 50 percent chance that the cat would be alive and a 50 percent chance that he would be dead, but this could not be proven until the cat's wave function collapsed, or until the box was opened. At that moment, two alternative universes would exist. The physicist gave a deranged grin. "And you will be in one of them," he added, pointing a finger at him for emphasis. Mingorance VI the Perplexed shuddered and couldn't help wondering whether at the same time as he was standing there confronting the abyss of the physicist's gaze, he wasn't simultaneously somewhere else, perhaps stepping gingerly into the widows' apartment, into a bleak alternative universe that reeked of boiled cauliflower. A terrible giddiness overwhelmed him as for an instant he saw himself duplicated, triplicated, quintuplicated, infinitely multiplied. He imagined how with each decision he took he had feverishly disseminated himself, frenetically spilled over, reproducing himself all day long like a rutting hamster, so that while he found himself in his neighbor's apartment, his own was teeming with a thousand other Mingorances, each going about their business, believing themselves unique and indivisible.

On his way back upstairs, he didn't even notice there was a tear in the packet and that he was leaving a trail of sugar behind him. Mingorance I the Irresolute all but knocked him down as two paramedics rushed down the stairs with him writhing on a stretcher. He entered the apartment behind Mingorance II the Intrepid, and the two men made their way to the kitchen, both keen to resolve the problem of the dratted coffee so that they could return to the living room and be exposed once more to the passionate gaze of Claudia, who was waiting for them under the blanket. They hurriedly brewed the requested potion as though vying to see who would finish first, and then assailed the woman with their respective trays. Claudia took a single sip and, snuggling back beneath the blanket, allowed herself to be comforted by those playful hands that were no longer seeking anything, except perhaps to steal her heart. Languid and trusting, she let them cradle her, certain that this stormy episode would last, that there would be no goodbyes or letters or unfulfilled promises, that he had an address where she could go if she wanted, a cozy nest where he would wait for her, hibernating, dream about her, yearn for her. How alive one feels with a beautiful woman in one's arms, how invincible, Mingorance II the Intrepid and Mingorance VI the Perplexed thought in unison, as the afternoon subsided amid an explosion of color that illuminated the blade of the *katana,* which at that moment Mingorance V the Untimely was hanging on the wall. Oblivious to Mingorance III the Brave shivering on the sofa beneath a blanket, Mingorance flung open the window, allowing an evocative smell of rain to engulf the apartment. Outside on the silent landing, two trails of sugar merged into a single sweet knot. From it emerged another track as thick as a rope, which slid beneath the door heading for the kitchen like a line of gunpowder in a fairy tale.

How dead one is inside an ambulance, how sadly anonymous we are, thought Mingorance I the Irresolute, writhing about. Coloring a few cats with red in its wake, the ambulance rode into the night toward the hospital, while death's dark fingers poked around inside him like a skilled mechanic. With the mask strapped to his face as if he were going to a carnival for consumptives, Mingorance I the Irresolute understood that it was entirely up to him whether he lived or died. And so, biting his lip, he confronted the pain and spasms with all the courage he could muster, and told himself over and over that if he didn't want to look foolish when explaining himself at the pearly gates, he must survive this self-inflicted act of catharsis. He knew he had triumphed in this duel with death as he crossed the threshold of the emergency ward. However, Mingorance VII the Weary had not been able to resist the tempting peace offered him by the Grim Reaper. Exhausted and disillusioned, he hadn't been able to refuse the irresistible invitation to throw down his cards on a game that was becoming increasingly stupid, possibly in the hope of beginning another with a fresh hand, perhaps finding himself more fortunate or courageous, even if he was reincarnated as a rat.

And while the putrefaction was being pumped out of Mingorance I the Irresolute's stomach through a desecrating tube, Mingorance was introducing into his, not without an air of reluctance, a spring roll that the Chinese waitress had just served him with calculated indifference. He had finally turned up to dine at the restaurant where he had renounced having lunch, but he was clear that this was the last time he would be eating at the Happy Panda. The waitresses' smoldering lack of friendliness seemed to have degenerated into resentment as the result of an attempted holdup earlier, while from his cushion the old Chinaman glared at him, eyes glowing like coals, as if he were the culprit, as if it was his hobby to set the West against him. The perfect end to a perfect day.

He finished his meal and fled the place before he burst into tears—something he couldn't help doing, although silently, discreetly, without making a scene—when he saw his neighbor wave to him triumphantly in the distance as he said goodbye to the redhead and went to carve another notch on his bedpost. Defeated, miserable, a failure in the eyes of the world, Mingorance climbed the stairs shedding silent tears, as if he were riding a scooter at high speed, pondering the many different ways there must be to spend a Saturday. He didn't even notice Mingorance II the Intrepid coming down with the redhead, carrying a bicycle and a dream.

Hearing the water from the shower—beneath which Mingorance VI the Perplexed, embracing himself ridiculously as he imagined he was still embracing Claudia, to whom he had just said goodbye without making another date, or exchanging telephone numbers, but with enough tenderness in his eyes to promise all of that—Mingorance considered taking a shower himself, but didn't feel he had the strength. Although it was only ten o'clock, he decided to go straight to bed, impatient to put an end to this fateful Saturday. He entertained the faint hope that on Sunday he would rise from that same bed as someone else, someone special, someone who knew how to do things differently. Soon after he lay down, Mingorance III the Brave came staggering over to the bed, perspiring and in a daze, fed up with waiting for the police, and also longing for that accursed Saturday to end. Five minutes later, having used up all the hot water and smelling of soap, they were

joined by Mingorance VI the Perplexed, followed by Mingorance IV the Abducted, who had seen a flying saucer but had
forgotten he had. Later, when Mingorance V the Untimely
grew tired of contemplating his *katana*, he also went to bed,
but only because he wanted to see it shine in his dreams.
Soon afterward, Mingorance I the Irresolute, who had just
come back from the hospital, from the foul stench of death,
collapsed onto the bed. Then it was the turn of Mingorance
II the Intrepid, who had been chain-smoking at the window,
watching his neighbor's apartment for the first time without
envy. Last to arrive, like a crow's feather alighting on a pot
of water, came the spirit of Mingorance VII the Weary. And
with every fresh arrival, Mingorance, teetering on the brink of
sleep, was aware of a pang in his soul each time he glimpsed
a parallel universe, a different Saturday from the one he had
experienced. He sensed that he had done other things unlike
those he had done, amassed experiences that would stay with
him like a warm residue, that he was simply the guiding thread
in a work of macramé, which was becoming interwoven with
other strands.

EPILOGUE

Sebastian Mingorance awoke on Sunday to glorious sun-
shine. He could scarcely believe his eyes when he drew back
the curtain. After a Saturday shrouded in clouds, the world

was shimmering beneath a resplendent sun. He smiled, tremendously relieved, because he knew that another day shut up at home would have made him reach for the reports or the rat poison. The trout could start trembling, because Mingorance was in the mood for fishing. After an invigorating shower, he got dressed and examined his tackle methodically.

He was checking the bait when a clatter of heels reached him from the landing. The sweet, slow music they made on the tiles led him to conjure up images of a beautiful woman perched on them. He assumed it must be an early customer of the seamstresses, who would continue her ascent, which is why the blood froze in his veins when the footsteps came to a halt outside his front door. He stopped what he was doing, gazing at the door with the expression of someone who has the kind of creditors that will break your fingers. Whoever it was, they appeared to be summoning the courage to ring the doorbell. Filled with curiosity, Mingorance crept catlike toward the door. Then he heard the brusque tearing of a page from a notebook, and seconds later watched incredulously as a note slipped between his waders. He picked it up and read the brief message: *I'm sorry, but you're not what I'm looking for.* Hearing the footsteps withdraw, and unable to understand what the note meant, he opened the door. Although her back was turned, he recognized her hair, and he detained her with a word, a name. Startled, she wheeled around and stared at him for a long while without saying anything. She would have blushed at realizing she was in the wrong building, if this man whom she could have sworn she had never seen before, and who was wearing a ridiculous hat adorned with trout flies, hadn't called her by her name. And he had said it so tenderly, as if they had spent the night together. Sebastian also looked at her in silence, unable to understand why, when he had tried to detain her to explain her mistake, he had used that particular name. It was as though a voice inside him had whispered it to him. Possibly the same voice that had kept him awake half the night, demanding incessantly that he go to an all-night supermarket halfway across the city to buy a bag of sugar.